"They've got him!" Tamara screamed from beneath Saraj's motionless body. "I saw them take Father away!"

Drewyn heard the police radio calling for interception and backup.

He turned and flew toward the Arth Mountains, as his father had said he should. There would be time to think—and to grieve—later, but not now.

"What are you doing?!" Tamara screamed. "*I don't want to go without him!* Make another attack!"

"Suicide," Drewyn said. "We'll be lucky to get away at all now. And if we can make it to Old Earth, you know that's what he'd want us to do."

"Want us to do? What does that have to do with it?!"

But she couldn't stop him; he wouldn't even answer her. She would have grabbed the controls from him if she'd known how, and if Saraj hadn't been sprawled helpless across her body.

"We can't leave him, Drewyn," she said in a pitiful voice. "You know we can't."

But her brother was flying hard, thinking only of escape.

BESTIARY MOUNTAIN

JOHN FORRESTER

A Starwanderer Book

Library of Congress Catalog Card Number: 86-45870

ISBN 0-694-05606-5

Published in hardcover by Bradbury Press,
an affiliate of Macmillan Publishing Co., Inc.
First Starwanderer edition, 1987.
Starwanderer books are published by
Harper & Row, Publishers, Inc.

For Rain

CONTENTS

BESTIARY MOUNTAIN

1 ⎯⎯⎯⎯⎯⎯⎯⎯⎯⎯⎯⎯⎯⎯⎯⎯

KANA

Kana closed the door of the chamber behind him and was blinded by darkness. The mountain was cold tonight, and he licked his lips and blinked into the northeast breeze. In a moment his cat's night vision was with him, and he felt better. He moved away from the doorseal in the rock — a possible target for his enemies — and turned his ears to listen.

When he was satisfied, he moved upward. Without his boots, the pads of his feet were cold on the smooth rocks, but the silence was worth the chill he felt. The ram could climb here faster than he, but never this quietly.

Soon he was on the highest level of the mountain, where each outcropping and ledge was washed in moonlight. He waited in a snag's shadow and studied the slopes far below him. The breeze was much too steady. It had been like this all day; a few more hours at this strength would bring poison from the Plains of Death.

A high white cloudbank drifted across the moon, and Kana took the dark moment to run down a well-kept trail through the woods to the far side of the mountain. He positioned himself for his watch there. He flexed his long claws, extending them from their sheaths, and made contact with the hard limestone surface beneath him. He almost wished for battle, rather than this endless waiting, night after night. It angered him that Tava would not tell what she was expecting, nor where her information came from. She sent him out to freeze and perhaps die each night; she trusted him to guard the castle-laboratories and all within the keep, but she held back secrets. She never spoke about her visits to the innermost chamber of the Round Beast, from which she would emerge a little dazed, drained and tired, and always bearing new knowledge.

Tava knew when to watch for attacks. She even knew the coming weather, the exact danger from passing death-storms or the distance to lethal rain. Since the Chemical Wars, which had destroyed civilization more than a hundred years past—at the turn of the twenty-first century—such had become the Knowledge of Life.

Suddenly Kana growled a single note as he smelled an animal. He crouched to the rock and focused his senses down the grade. The little wafts of air that curled over the mountain and returned upslope brought it to him again. No question—this was the ram, rank and fresh. He wasn't more than half a mile away. Kana felt his heart beating inside his chest, and he wished he could silence the harsh undertone of his breathing. It was too late to run for a doorseal and warn Tava. Kana's ears lay flat against his head.

Come to the cat then, ram, he thought.

As if Kana had called his enemy out loud, the ram bounded up the steep mountainside. He was running in a straight line, wasting no energy, locked on and guided by some device—heat sensing or radar—something, because the ram's nose wasn't this good. It was frightening to see him run so fast and hear the sharp clapping of his hooves on the rock. His massive, curved horns reflected the moonlight as if they were varnished.

The ram covered his last hundred yards so fast that Kana's resolve was broken; he felt helpless before the thunderbolt. The final leap to Kana's boulder seemed instantaneous, and the impact knocked him flying backward through the dark, cold air. He gasped for breath as he fell and crashed through the sharp branches of a pine, landing hard on the bones of his back. He rolled over slowly as icy air seeped once more into his chest.

The ram had leapt high from the boulder and was skidding in soft, shallow dirt, his eyes suddenly inadequate to the light. For an instant he stood near Kana in the pine-shadow, whipping his great head from side to side, filled with the catscent but unsure where to strike. Kana sprang to his back, raking long, unsheathed claws deeply along the ram's wide shoulders. Then the cat flew upward into the thickety pine, clutching and climbing. He felt like a terrified squirrel.

Below him the ram was spinning, turning nimbly with gasping pain-breaths as if he thought the cat was still aboard his bleeding shoulders. Kana almost fell on him again, but his man-half clutched the tree instead, resisting the instinct. He smelled ram's blood and his stomach knotted for the leap, but it was already too late. His enemy was running down the slope.

My hesitation! Kana thought bitterly, digging his claws into the bark and meat of the pine. He hissed and spit and tore at the tree.

Then he climbed down and walked, slowly and upright, to the brow of the mountain. He trembled and sucked in the cold air, grateful his lungs would fill again. His chest hurt; there would be a bad bruise. But his heart was almost calm now, and the ram would not be back tonight. A shiver passed through him . . . something he felt for his blood-enemy. *Sympathy? For those claw-rakes that saved my life? Do I not wish the ram's death?* he asked himself. *But why not?* Confusion began to rise in him, and he stopped it with a smooth, deliberate act of mind. His cat's repose settled over him. He knew it was a blanket he perhaps shouldn't use. After all, it was the man-thoughts, the incessant worrying, that had come to rule creation, while cats evolved as their house pets, or as outlandish wild beasts who had become "endangered" — the old word — and then disappeared from the earth.

Kana took his time returning to the doorseal, allowing himself the impassive and satisfied walk of his cat-ancestors. He reached the keep and hesitated at the door. The breeze was fresh and clean, and mercifully it had shifted around to the west. Its coldness thrilled him. Inside, he would be merely the servant again. *Is that what I am?* he wondered. *Or Tava's pet? Or soldier?* His heart was sad. Out here he felt lord of Bestiary Mountain. But inside, what? What?

2 ———————————————

Through the clear dome, Tamara Langstrom watched a line of light cruisers crossing the sky of the moon. She wondered which was piloted by her brother, and which by his friend Jaric. She and Drewyn, twins and telepaths, were 16 now, and Jaric was 18. Soon he would graduate from Spaceforce training and be sent to far moonside for two years of right-think instruction, the beginning of an officer's life. Drewyn would remain here that long — learning the skills of flying and laser war, as well as the old-fashioned ones of karate and fencing. Even so, she wouldn't see much of her brother from this time on. She turned her eyes bitterly from the sky.

Across the smooth expanse of green marble that was the lyceum's center, she caught a glimpse of a long, silken robe — chocolate brown — the figure of an Overone watching her again.

Would they never let up? She quickly took a path to the right and hurried through the air lock into the huge greenhouse. A thousand yards high, a mile across, constructed of triple-thick glassamyer, it was dense as a jungle with the last of Old Earth's surviving flora. Deep in its bamboo forests, among breadfruit trees, lemons and limes, orchids and roses, Tamara had found a favorite place to escape the Overones, meditate and think. And most of all to breathe. Here was the real air of Old Earth, fresh from the plants, the life-giving oxygenation her lungs were made for, evolved and bred over eons on the planet she had never touched, never seen except as a giant luminescent moon in the true moon's night sky, a ball floating in the blue haze of ash and dust from the final wars.

She slipped into an exhibit of elephant-leaf philodendron and sat on the hidden rock in its center. Even if the Overone followed her inside the greenhouse, she wouldn't find her without electronic-search, and she'd need permission for that. Tamara's grades were straight Alphas, her athletic marks high enough and she had only the slightest record of social deviance. Caught twice outside the dormpound after hours—once with her brother, once with Jaric—she had been detained, interrogated and almost polygraphed. That would have fixed them all. But her standing was strong, her secret unguessed. If the Overones knew her real reasons for being out those nights, she would be branded a criminal already, and the merest suspicion by an Overone would be enough for electronic-search of the greenhouse or anywhere else.

Tamara closed her eyes and breathed slowly and deeply. The cool, rich air poured in and all through her body. She could think most clearly here, reveling in the old secrets of yoga-breath, of mind-calming and of thought-ordering, taught by her father. She would need them all for what had to be done soon.

There was the soft click of the greenhouse door closing. Tamara listened, motionless and focused. The Overone?

And what if she were caught here? It was not strictly against rules to spend time in Luna's greenhouses, but it was considered archaic and sentimental in a dangerous way, like visiting the zoo past the age of twelve. Too much feeling for plants and animals was something to be watched, according to the guardians of Overstory. Humankind had conquered the animals in the final wars that came after genetic engineering had given animals minds and hands, and the correct attitude of victor to vanquished was one of smugness and pity, not the lingering affection often found in Underones. There was even a movement now to destroy the last remaining specimens in the zoos, lest they ever rise again. But greenhouses and zoos still served a purpose—to impress upon each new generation the unsavory past on Old Earth. As humanoid engineering improved all the time, approaching the ideal height, weight and IQ, the animals were thought to become uglier and uglier. "There is the swamp of your past!" the guides shouted at schoolchildren. "Give thanks for genetic engineering and the future!" Those children who came back on their own time to linger in the zoos and greenhouses were observed and recorded in Overstory's permanent files. There were likely candidates for the sulfur pits and the iron and cinnabar mines, maybe even for the hated industrial cities in space.

But Tamara had been chosen for better things. She would soon be enrolled in the guardian school of Station VII, separated from "ordinary" boys and girls her age; and if she excelled as expected, she might not meet Drewyn or Jaric until years later, when she could possibly confront them as their political ruler, making decisions to send them forth, two among countless warriors on conquest voyages into deep space.

There was a footstep near the exhibit where Tamara hid, and she held her breath.

Silence. *Trying to outwait me*, she thought.

Tamara calmed herself, breathed deeply and entered the first stage of self-trance, another of the forbidden skills her father had taught her.

Time drifted by, and finally there was an impatient shuffle and a sliding of silk, the crunch of a step on fine stones, and the door clicked shut again.

Tamara slipped out between the wide leaves and sought another door. She pulled her helmet down and fastened it, adjusted the pressure, then loped in long, graceful bounds through the light lunar gravity, across the space of marble toward her dormpound. She felt refreshed and proud of herself for the small victory. *What a dreadful fate* they *have*, she thought, *to go through all that training—lyceum and guardian school—and then have to serve as apprenticedeans, checking up on suspicious young people*. She did not believe, in that moment, it could be her fate as well.

She entered the astrodome that contained her own building and hurried to her room. She was supposed to be completing a report on the history of self-reference problems in mathematics, an advanced project for her age but one she enjoyed. She was a little behind schedule, though, because of her far more secret studies and the energy they took from her nights.

Once inside her room she pulled off her S-suit and hung it in the closet with her helmet. She turned on her computer, opened the math file and began to review her notes.

Suddenly the modem began to flash.

She pulled out the math disk and replaced it with a blank, then translated as the code line appeared.

MEET ME AT TEN, MOON BEAUTY, it read.

She smiled and blushed. She was tempted to tease Jaric,

just to be coy; she wanted to trade messages and elicit another compliment. But it was too risky. So she just punched in an affirmative and erased the whole exchange from the machine's memory. She knew she was being monitored more and more closely as lyceum graduation drew near, and it was time to work out a new code. There were forces among the Overones that would try to prevent any Langstrom from entering guardian school.

Tamara replaced the math disk and sighed. *Moon Beauty. That Jaric. What a beauty* he *is,* she thought. *Tall and relaxed, with a long face full of warmth, usually on the verge of a smile when he isn't thinking of the trainers, and with those brown eyes. The worst thing about my being so special,* she thought, *about being chosen for guardianship, is losing Jaric.*

She closed her eyes and saw him as he was two nights ago, sitting with her in the desert sand of the station on Moon Island V. Here, in this space station permanently orbiting Luna, the animals bred in moon labs had been released for hunting by the workers. There had been lion-rams and rhino-buffalo, tigers with horns, anything the geneticists could dream up and splice together out of DNA. That program was fading out now, and only a few of the old dune bears were left, but Island V wasn't just the home of the last fugitive game-creatures. It was also home to Luna's only outlaw, Ryland Langstrom, Tamara's father.

Here she and Drewyn and Jaric came on their midnight flights, fooling all the moon security systems so far, to visit and study with Ryland.

And here, two nights past, when the lessons in mind control were over, she had spent an hour on the dark sands with Jaric. There was no starry sky above, because the giant station was in a spin duplicating Old Earth's gravity, and a dome of glassamyer that was transluscent would have presented spinning streaks of light and made its passengers sick. So the glassamyer, hybrid of glass and steel, stronger than the finest earth-steel and spun from pure single crystals in vacuum factories aboard spacecraft, was tinted to screen out the light. The nights were utterly black, except for the spotlights deep inside Ryland's cave. The Overones suspected he was still at large on Island V, and they could have cut its life-support systems to flush him out or kill him. But he had shown them, over the years, that he would harm no one, that his only wish was to study the remaining beasts of that colony-world. Once they had tried a search-and-destroy to get him, and he had shown them what his retaliation could be. He'd descended to the moon's surface in a small cruiser disguised as a repair vehicle and wrecked millions of dollars worth of projects in a single night. The robot water-walkers were an especially easy target. These machines marched along the terminator—the line between frozen night and blazing day on the lunar surface, straddling the 500-degree temperature difference, sensing the choicest hydrous rocks strewn about there. A shovel would pick up a rock on the daylight side, crush and heat it to 1,200 degrees in a self-contained solar furnace. The process would release the water vapor into a compartment, and at this moment the water-walker would cross into the night side of the terminator where the vapor would condense by natural refrigeration. From there, the water would be brought back to Industrial Central, decomposed by electrolysis, then transformed into liquid oxygen and hydrogen; these substances were the basis of lunar survival, from portable backpacks to the giant systems powering astrodomes, underground cities and orbiting stations. Ryland had taken his revenge by lasering a dozen of these expensive robots, then he'd left a note in Central, where they'd never suspected he could enter. LET US LEAVE EACH OTHER ALONE, it had said, and, so far, they had done it.

But there were signs that they were tired of the truce and would come for him soon. And if the truth were known, Ryland was in no shape to resist. His food was running out. In these last months before Tamara, Jaric and Drewyn were each sent off to their separate schools, they had been slipping into Island V late at night, smuggling Ryland supplies.

Jaric had taken Tamara's hand between his own warm hands, bent down and kissed her.

"I've got a surprise for you," he'd said.

"Hmmm?"

"I got permission from your father to tell you."

She strained in the darkness to see whether he was teasing her.

"When graduation comes this time . . ."

"Yes?"

"Well, I'm not letting you go. That's one thing."

She laughed. "And how are you going to change things? Just ask the Overones in a polite voice? Uh, excuse me, First Gorid of all Overones, but I want you to bend the rules for a friend of mine."

"Very funny, Tamara," he'd said, squeezing her shoulder gently.

"I've got it," she said. "We've decided we don't want to be a warrior and a guardian. Just ship us out to the cinnabar mines, and we'll be good little slaves for you the rest of our lives."

He made a grim sound, almost laughing.

"No, listen," he said. "It's much better than that. You know we've talked with your father about stealing a ship and taking off for Old Earth."

She grew very still. "Yes."

"Well, he's been working on the plan, Tamara. In minute detail."

"Jaric—"

"I'm not kidding."

"I don't know, Jaric. It scares me."

"Your father is sure we can do it."

"We always joke about 'when we go to Old Earth.'"

"Not this time."

"I wish I could *see* you," she said, pinching his arms, "so I'd know what expression is on your sorry face."

But he was silent.

"Your mother did it."

"Maybe. They say she went off course and drifted out into space."

"They? Overones? Your father doesn't believe that, and neither do I."

Tamara was quiet for a while, thinking in the darkness. This was too much for her to completely believe, and besides, Jaric was always kidding about something. She tried to picture them doing it, but all she could think of was how utterly strange Old Earth would be.

"Imagine," she finally said. "Earth-g all the time."

"Yeah," he said, raising his arm, feeling it.

"You know," Tamara said, "I come out here to visit Father, or I go up to Island II for my exercise class, and I don't think that much about earth gravity. I mean, it's strange, and I guess it's good for us to work out in the resistance . . . but to think about *never* doing moon loping again . . . know what I mean?"

"Yeah. The worst thing, for me, would be losing my place on the aerosoccer team."

She nodded, imagining him on the weightless station, wearing his arm and leg fins, actually flying in the thick of the game. "That would be hard to give up, wouldn't it?"

"Yes, Tamara. But it will probably be worth it, to gain your company."

"Probably?"

He laughed and pulled away but not before she hit him in the stomach. Then they tussled with each other. When they were still again, in each other's arms, they heard Drewyn's low whistle.

"Hey!" he whisper-yelled. "Time to go."

They started back, hand in hand, and she said, "I'm not sure I believe a word of this Old Earth business, Jaric."

"Suit yourself," he said, grinning as they came into the lights of Ryland's cave. Then he put his finger to his lips, reminding her that all he'd said was a secret. Now she really was confused and not sure whether she should discuss it with Ryland and Drewyn. Anyway, there hadn't been time. Hurriedly they'd climbed aboard the light cruiser, waved good-bye to Ryland and headed for the locks in the center of Island V that would release them into the airless nightspace high above the moon.

Tamara had made it back safely to her dormpound. That night she dreamed of really stealing a ship and flying to Old Earth. But in the dream she was alone, and she landed hard in a dark forest. She wandered through tangled willows and beeches and other trees from books looking for her mother, sensing her in the deep ferns and thickets. And she was always just ahead, just ahead.

Since then, for the last two days, Tamara had tried to

keep the escape idea out of her mind, feeling almost that the Overones would know she was thinking of it. But tonight with Jaric beside her again, feeling his warm presence, she'd make him stop teasing her about this and tell the whole truth.

3

THE DUNE BEARS

High above the moon's surface in the desert of Island V, Bjorn and his mate and their last cub loped across the red dunes toward their cave. Again they had found no food, only the bones of their tribesmen blanched and parching on the sands. It had been many days—beyond their counting—since they had eaten. And they had seen no living kin in all that time.

They reached the cliff and began to climb. It surprised Bjorn that his cub still stayed. The other one had given up days ago, when the light-beasts had fired upon them. Bjorn's foreleg kept bleeding, and it was swollen and aching from the hole. He dragged himself upward by three massive legs and barred his teeth to the wind, growling as he pictured the thin light-beasts again. Without their barking sticks that put the little holes in others they would be helpless.

Bjorn kept climbing without turning his head. He couldn't help his mate and cub now, if they failed to follow him. But he heard them when he controlled his breathing. His claws found footing in the loose rock and blue clay, and he knew the lair was just a little higher.

Then he saw the shadow of the home-ledge above him

and knew he would not freeze on the mountain's face. All
his kinsmen had frozen—even his other cub—and he
could not imagine what it meant. But they would not
move again, no matter how he nudged and nuzzled. They
lay without breathing, and their eyes changed to rock in
just the time of digging-a-beetle. Then they let the wind
and the small-beasts work their hides away. Before it was
over, only white bones remained, and, after the new-cub
time, most of these would be gone.

Bjorn made the ledge. Soon he and his family were in
their cave, all the way back, and they lay down together.
As the fur-warmth grew over them and the aching of the
wound subsided, Bjorn thought of all his hunting lands
one by one, seeing their emptiness and his missing
brother's old tracks in each place. There was no life
without hunting, but there was no use in trying again.
Back and forth Bjorn's thoughts swam, as his mate's fur-
heat spread through him, and his eyes grew helpless and
heavy. He heard the cub crying as he fell asleep.

Then there was a light at the mouth of the cave, and
something moving there.

Bjorn rumbled awake, half inside an eating-dream
still, and he was staring and fighting the leg-aching as he
stood drinking in the other-smell, the enemy-close smell.
He roared and pushed his mate and cub aside, charging
on three legs toward the circle of light.

The light-beast-shape dodged outside, out of sight.
Bjorn stopped short of the entrance, trying to decide. In
front of him was a dead rabbit. And a bundle of corn ears
tied together. Enemy-anger and food-yes flashed
together, jumped against each other in Bjorn's brain. His
mate tried to rush past him toward the meat, but he
growled at her and she held. Once the light-beasts had

tried to trick them with an offering. That time the clan had eaten well and then sticks had begun to bark from far away, and two kin-brothers had frozen. So Bjorn himself approached the rabbit, sniffing and turning it, watching the cave-mouth all the time. He made to grab the rabbit, then drew into the stance for battle. Again and again he tested this unseen enemy, waiting for the rush and the fight to death. Finally he was only conscious of the rabbit's crazing smell, and his memories of death-fights in the past. It was the cub who broke the waiting at last— Bjorn knew it was time when he saw the boy seizing the corn through his own haze of exhaustion; his ritual of outwaiting had left him too tired to truly keep watch or to control his family. It no longer mattered whether this was an ambush. They had to eat what lay there in front of them.

As they ate, Doctor Ryland Langstrom watched. He had no idea they called him a "light-beast," after the sun's reflection on his hairless skin, just as the big male had no thought that the man called him "Bjorn." Proper names among the bears were a matter of individual smells, and only the rare clan leader achieved a special, descriptive grunt-sound to mark its presence.

The man knew this, as he knew so much more about the bears. Their creation, from grizzly-stock in the Old Earth cell banks, was an experiment in cryogenic suspension, a mix of the basic creature with human brain DNA to increase intelligence—an experiment undertaken for sport.

The Betas and even lower-level humanoids who managed and worked the sulfur pits and crystal factories and cinnabar mines needed a release from their cramped and angry lives. The Overones had come upon this plan, solidly based on Old Earth accounts of deer hunting as a safety valve for millions of low-paid workers, and they had created the dune bears in their genetic laboratories.

The researchers had tried different levels of intelligence-enhancing injections, but they had been sloppy about recording the dosages, since these were only sport-creations, like the giant eagle-ducks of the generation before. Those had been an incredible success with shooters, increasing productivity in hunters' factories by a full third, and a resale market for the mounted birds had gone wild. Of course, the tragedy was in killing them all off, assuming the labs could always produce more. But it hadn't worked out that way. It seemed the gene-code patterns hadn't been recorded with complete perfection. Though there were still government grants available for any geneticists willing to try, no more eagle-ducks had been produced. There was more money in organic-robot design.

The bears were about to follow the eagle-ducks into nonexistence, and, except for the hunters, Doctor Ryland Langstrom was the only human who cared.

He lay on the flat rock fifty yards out from the cave mouth, suspended on the edge of the mountain over the red desert far below, and with his infrared binoculars watched Bjorn, his mate and their famished cub. Ryland was barely surviving himself, and he knew he could never feed the animals from his own subsistence food supply. But if these bear-creatures were intelligent enough to trust him and if he were lucky, they all might live a bit longer, and he might learn a certain secret from them: he wanted to know if they would sacrifice for each other.

"Come on, Bjorn," he whispered, "relax and think

about what I've done. I don't have any more food to spare, and I can't think of what more I could do or say to you, to make you realize."

It wasn't in Ryland's nature to grieve for lost causes, even that of his own life. Tava had been the same way. And as he lay on the cold rock watching the feeding shapes in the bear-cave, he thought how proud she would be of him now.

She was such a beautiful woman, and the day he had proposed — on their break from Biology II in the first year of guardian school — she had grown quiet and focused her gray eyes. "What about the animals?" she had said.

"Uh, what, Tava?"

Then she had smiled so that he felt helpless. "Come to my dormpound tonight," she said.

Tava had insisted on a pact.

And they agreed on their devotion to restoring the plants and animals of Old Earth, and to respecting the new creatures, the combined animal-human hybrids that Tava felt had just as much right to live as the ancient kinds.

It had been his idea to have one child, manageable with their work, which had turned out as the twins, Drewyn and Tamara.

But when the chance for an escape-ship to Old Earth came, a chance to see if there really was life there — as Overstory said there was not — Tava had looked him clearly in the eyes and been ready to remind him of their promises.

But it hadn't been necessary. He took her in his arms for the last time, and then they hugged the baby twins between them for a long hour. When the adventurous students who had stolen the unlikely shuttlecraft finally came and hurried away with Tava, Ryland had begun his long and private mourning for her and the life of dedicated work they had dreamed of together. He kept records on the eagle-ducks, as he listened to the shotguns bringing their last members down into the marshes. As he made notes and listened for his twins to cry in the night, and thought of his future without his beautiful wife, Ryland Langstrom had tried to imagine the years to come.

But that was for a young man with a smooth and innocent face. Now with his children cut off from him by the government, and his last research project about to vanish into the *nada* of the bears' senseless extinction, Ryland tried to decide what he should do. Surely the hunters with their laser rifles would soon come. And when they did, the bears would have nowhere to run.

Ryland stood up and very slowly started walking toward the mouth of the cave.

4

AN OVERONE ACCUSER

Tamara found Saraj in the library poring over a book on marine life, dreaming of the seas of Old Earth before the war. It was a quality she loved Saraj for, this brooding about their ancestral planet, and the sort of interest the Overones hated. Saraj was to graduate from the lyceum along with Tamara, but that would be the end of her formal education. She would be married to a mineworker in the Iron Range or to a caver in the sulfur mountains or, if she were very lucky, to a young warrior/explorer. She was not considered bright enough for guardianship, being only a Beta-minus student, and she had a dreamy way that the Overones detested. She was Tamara's roommate in the dormpound, and Tamara suspected this was an arranged match to keep her out of trouble. It was probably thought that Saraj would "understimulate her roving and challenging tendencies," as they would put it—her greatest career obstacle.

"Hi," Tamara said, looking over Saraj's shoulder at a picture of a blue whale, an extinct monster of the old oceans.

"Oh, hi. Just look at her, Tamara. This is a female—they're the ones that grew so large. Isn't she beautiful?

Someday I'll get into the Library of Sound and hear her songs."

"If they let you," Tamara said quietly.

"Yeah," Saraj said with a long sigh, closing the book reluctantly.

She was a small girl with a pretty face, sad blue eyes and long red hair. Freckles spread across her light skin.

Tamara put her arm around her friend's shoulders as they walked together to the dining hall. Tamara was taller, with brown hair worn straight and long like Saraj's, in defiance of the approved style, which was medium-length and curled.

They sat together, lost among the hundreds of girls at the long tables, and ate their caulifungus soup while they listened to the lecture.

Tonight it was about the glories of the hydroponic fungus farms, the fresh varieties of foodstuffs appearing almost daily from the Center for Genetic Surgery, and the increasing amount of oxygen these new crops were breathing into the astrodome skies. Tamara didn't have to be told that—looking out through any of the transparent airdomes, the atmospheric change was obvious in the ever-deepening sunrise and sunset colors, and in the sight of an ever-widening earth on low-horizon.

After the droning speech and the boring soup, the two girls walked together to their room in the dormpound, rolling their eyes as they passed loud and silly classmates in the halls. Giggling and towel-fighting now, these innocents would soon draw their post-grad assignments, either one-child or sterilization, depending on the grades they were making now.

Reaching their room, Tamara opened the door and jumped at what she saw. There sat the Overone from the greenhouse, legs crossed beneath her chocolate silk robe and fingers drumming on her cheek. "Close the door, girls," she said.

"You're a young one, aren't you?" Tamara said. "Just graduate or what?"

"Impertinent," the Overone snapped.

"Not necessarily," Tamara said. "They're sending me to that school, too, and it's very pertinent to *me* what kind of women it turns out!"

"Sit down," the Overone said angrily.

Tamara and Saraj sat on the edge of Tamara's bed.

"Now, Tamara Langstrom, did you receive a modem transmission this afternoon?"

The Overone watched her eyes.

"Yes," she said. "As a matter of fact, it was right after I'd started work. Some strange signal, or feedback. Something. I couldn't figure it out."

"I see. You couldn't figure it out. Did you report it?"

"Uh, no—I forgot it right away, until this minute! But I'm reporting it now, to you. Okay?"

"Certainly not," the Overone said coldly. "Did you send a message in response?"

"No . . . I mean, I typed something, just some letters, to see if the feedback would clear up. . . ." *She doesn't look like a bad soul*, Tamara thought. *How do they get them to act so mean in that school*? Undoubtedly it had something to do with celibacy . . . ten long years of it after lyceum. . . .

"Your transmissions were monitored on Master Unit III, Ms. Langstrom. Would you like to give me the code key for them now?"

"Code? Honestly," Tamara said, glancing at Saraj with the most relaxed smile she could manage. At this moment Tamara was grateful she had never confided her message system to her friend.

"You deny receiving an actual communication?" the Overone demanded.

"Of course I do. Unless it was something I missed. As I said, I was mapping Gödel numbers — my math project — and —"

"You will live to regret this moment, if you are lying," the Overone said as she rose.

"No doubt," Tamara said. "However, since I'm telling you all I know about the matter . . ."

"We shall see," the woman said, walking haughtily from the room.

When the door shut, Tamara fell back on Saraj's bed.

"What did you do?" Saraj asked.

"You will live to regret this moment . . ." Tamara mocked with witch's hands and a leer. The girls laughed together. "I didn't do anything," Tamara finally said. "That creep! Did you ever see such a creep in your life?"

Saraj swallowed and hesitated. "No," she whispered, "I never did."

The girls studied until lights-out at nine-thirty, and once Saraj seemed asleep, Tamara prepared to sneak out. She wasn't sure what her friend knew about her activities, but she felt it was better for Saraj to be as innocent as possible, in case she was ever scanned.

Tamara slipped to the roof, using the keys Jaric had made for her in astronautics shop, then she jumped high over the electronic grid and crossed to the far side.

She climbed up the wall of a solar collector and watched the domesky.

At precisely ten, a light cruiser, operating illegally and in darkness, flew up beside her and hovered.

The aft dome lifted and she scrambled aboard.

But the pilot was her brother, not Jaric.

Heart sinking, she started to ask where he was.

"Shhhh—" Drewyn said.

Knowing he feared voicescan, she nodded and strapped on her seatbelt. The lift was sudden and wonderful.

In moments they were shooting across the moonsky, just underneath the dome itself—*while all the other girls are locked in the dormpound*, Tamara thought, gazing at scattered lights in the black plain below.

They reached the holding lock, and there was no one ahead of them.

Drewyn entered a code series on his panel—a brilliant system Jaric had devised for masquerading as an official mailship—and the lockbay slid open. Soon they were released into the spacesky beyond, breathing cabin oxygen, and free to talk.

Drewyn shot the cruiser straight up into the darkness, and Tamara grinned as she felt herself mashed back against her seat.

"At last!" she said loudly.

"Good to be out of there?"

"So good! Fly this thing faster! I want to scream out loud! And where is Jaric? The message I got was from him."

"One thing at a time," he said, leveling off on a course for the red desert colony of Island V.

"Nothing's wrong is it?" she asked.

"They caught Jaric sending the message," Drewyn said. "He wouldn't admit what it was, but they've got him under brainscan right this minute."

5 ———————————————

A GOOD DEATH

Bjorn and his family had finished the rabbit and the corn when the light-beast appeared in the cave's mouth. Bjorn growled low in his throat and moved steadily toward the ugly thing, realizing each second that something was different. The stick! There was no barking stick, unless it was hidden behind the thin, almost hairless body.

The light-beast held up a single paw and made calm noises in its throat. They were deeper than Bjorn would have expected—this must be a male. *Perhaps they are to lull me*, Bjorn thought. He came on and on, until the light-beast's rank smell was full-with-him, forcing his lips back in the foul-sneer, and yet the thing made no move to attack or to defend itself. Bjorn rose suddenly on two great hind legs and raised his one good arm for the kill. The frail creature still stood its ground, senselessly waiting to be frozen. *So be it then*, Bjorn thought, *so be it*. He was coming down with all his strength when the light-beast jumped back and produced from behind him a single ear of corn. Bjorn held off a moment, staring and trying to see it turn into a barking stick. But it gave the corn-smell, as it should.

The light-beast tossed it at Bjorn's feet, and he waited.

Why does one enemy come this way to die? Bjorn asked himself. He circled the light-beast, which remained still and calm, and moved to the cliff's edge. The breeze was strong and cold, and the dunes far below seemed empty. Bjorn's eyes were tight; he thought perhaps distant sticks would speak and he would feel another hole, but nothing happened.

Angry at these decisions that were forced upon him when he was wounded and starving, he moved again toward the stinking light-beast and looked into its tiny eyes. *Perhaps, then, the beast itself means to be our food, after the rabbit and the corn. Perhaps this is something we never knew about them, the way they choose to stop moving. Instead of being frozen and feeding the small-beasts, they disappear all at once into the bodies of their enemies.* Bjorn slowly circled it and backed into the cave where his mate was waiting.

The cub rushed up to the light-beast first and stood for a moment, trembling and sniffing its legs in confusion. Then the light-beast reached out with its naked white paw and petted the big cub between his ears. It was a motion so unplanned, so smooth-flowing and kinlike, that it saved the light-beast's life. Both Bjorn and his mate stopped then, helpless before this ancient and familiar gesture, not grasping why they were unable to kill.

Then the light-beast amazed them again. He eased down on all fours and rolled over on his back, exposing his soft side and throat to the excited cub. The cub jumped on him now, tugging with his claws and hugging the light-beast with his powerful short legs and growling the play-growl he hadn't uttered in so long.

As quickly as it had begun, the wrestling ended. The cub was too hungry to use its energy this way, and it

walked to its mother, whining and shaking its head.
Bjorn divided the last ear of corn and gave it to them.

Seeing that, the man had a good part of the answer he
had almost died to get. He had thought these dune bears
were capable of sacrifice, but watching them cooperate
with each other when times were good was no proof.
Now, though, seeing this magnificent male, clan leader
bereft of his clan, giving up his bit of dried corn in spite
of his own starvation and pain from the rifle wound . . .
this was all the proof anyone could want.

Ryland knew the bears must die soon. With this final
observation on their moral growth, his notes were almost
complete. No scientific paper would ever carry what he
knew into the next generation, for the government allowed no such studies anymore. But he had a practical
hope for his work, much better than recognition by a
jury of professors.

He stayed in his place against the wall of the cave.

The bears watched him for an hour, during which he
avoided meeting and challenging their eyes. Then, as if
he had been a rock formation, they ignored him. They
moved to the back of their cave and slept in a warm heap
together, and Ryland stretched his legs and dozed. He
woke with the cub's nose on his cheek, and its snuffling-
rooting sounds in his ears. Gradually, he crossed his legs
and took the lotus position, slowing his heartbeat for the
long wait.

The bears moved around very little; they seemed to be
sleeping as much as possible. Ryland guessed they had
despaired of finding food. This was another sign of their
intelligence, for he knew what they could not—the rabbits and rodents of their foraging, the occasional deer
and even the seemingly endless supply of beetles and the

rotten logs that housed them—all had been supplied for the dune bears by the government that created and, for a time, chose to sustain them.

During the night Bjorn awoke with a sickening streak coming and going through his body. He rose and waited for his head to clear, but the dizziness stayed with him. He moved to the thing-that-smelled and stood over it a long time, no longer concerned for the threat-of-it, but wishing it gone from his home. He poked it gently with his good foreleg, and finally it roused from what seemed long-sleep. Bjorn pointed to the cave mouth then and grunted to the hairless beast. It first tried to ignore the poking and prodding, but when Bjorn added a single claw to the message it stood right up.

"Grrrrraahhhhhhh!" Bjorn said. *Find your own home.* The light-beast seemed to understand. It left the cave. And at last fresh air began its slow, cleansing work.

The bear returned to his warm mate and cub and lay down with them. His dreams were full of big, soft logs with beetles crunchy and sweet, and he drifted through a green-corn field under a mild sky. Then the barking began. At first it was dream-barking and fear-testing, but then he was standing up feeling new holes all over him, the warm liquid running down his chest and his legs not-supporting. He was more surprised than panicked, and he felt his mate and cub with him jerked backward deeper and deeper into the cave wall. *The light-beasts with their barkers*, he thought. *Their cowards' barkers and their night-trick on us here. Thankful I'm not them*, Bjorn felt as he sank down. *Thankful I'm not them. So-this-is-to-be-frozen, this-is-to-be-frozen, this-is-to-be-frozen, this-is-to-find-out.*

6 ━━━━━━━━━━━━━━━━━━━━

LAST RENDEZVOUS

●

The light cruiser shot across spacesky in the lunar night.

"Seven minutes to the V lockbay," Drewyn said.

"Tell me about Jaric."

"They decoded his message an hour ago — and grabbed him down the hall from his room. He was on the phone with me or *I* wouldn't even know."

"Are you sure that's the reason they took him?"

"Almost positive. I loped across the training runway and watched the lighted windows. They jerked him along all the way to Central Research. You know what's in there."

Tamara dug her nails into her hands and studied the unblinking jewel stars, wasting seconds in blind thoughtless frustration. She closed her eyes and visualized Jaric, just for a passing instant, and he was indeed strapped to a table and wired. Her eyes sprung back to the green phospor lights of the control panel.

"Let's get him out," she said quickly.

"We will."

"Haven't you passed the compound already?"

"We're going to meet Father first."

Tamara blushed in anger.

"I want him out as badly as you do," Drewyn snapped. "But Father will know—"

"Just how to do it? Did you think about consulting me?"

"Look," he said. "I'm piloting the ship. Jaric is my blood brother."

"Your what?"

"I didn't mean to say that. He's my best friend. If there was more time, sure I'd ask you. Anyway, you know Father's expecting us. He'd be worried to death if we just left him in the desert with no word."

"How can we ever get Jaric out?" The chill was beginning to reach her—they'd never penetrate security.

"I've got an idea." Drewyn gave a quick, full grin. Tamara sank in her seat. She knew he was very smart, but his confidence now seemed strange, maybe dangerous.

"Well?"

"Wait till we speak with Father."

Tamara stared out on the spacenight, her arms crossed tightly.

Soon they reached the lockbay, and Drewyn hovered their craft delicately in its holding dock, fins quivering while he ran the computer password code, and just as smoothly as before they were admitted.

In a moment they were accelerating again, this time low over the red desert, and Drewyn was blazing full searchlights on the dunes. She didn't question his piloting— he must need the light to avoid hitting a tree or a stone peak. Suddenly they shot over a party of men. They were carrying rifles and something huge on a dragsled, and for the instant Tamara saw their frightened faces in the aerial glare. Then the little cruiser was well past them, traveling the direction they had come, and Drewyn was slowing for his landing.

"Something's wrong!" Tamara cried as the desert rose to meet them.

They skidded in the soft red sandust and came to a stop. Tamara unlatched her cover and quickly climbed up, then jumped from the cruiser. She ran toward her father's cave, smelling smoke in the darkness and flashing on images of destruction.

She rounded the boulders and there it was, a black, smoking mouth lit dimly by embers. It had been blasted out, gutted by fire; smoke trailings leaked from the opening.

"Father?" she called softly.

The cool breeze twisted up the smoke and dragged it across her.

There was only silence. Tamara saw them in her mind, men with lasers standing here within the hour, spewing long snakes of green light-fire into the cave.

Drewyn took her arm and held it tightly.

CHOSEN OF OVERONES HIGH

Saraj was dreaming when the pulser went off. Implanted beneath her skin, it throbbed like a wild second heartbeat and drove her crazy. She jumped up in the darkness, squeezed her arm where it moved and hurried out the door to meet them.

They had never used it before; it was only for emergencies. She found the haughty brownrobe who had interrogated Tamara standing downstairs and, without a word, followed her to the waiting light cruiser. Soon she had left the world of schoolgirls far behind.

The pilot flew fast across the moonsurface and entered the high security airlocks without giving any signal that Saraj could see. Just as she expected, they landed before the glassamyer, fortress-like building, and the pilot pressed a computer key that lifted the cockpit's dome. He never spoke. They were admitted, and Saraj followed the Overone to the big elevator, closed her eyes against the sudden fall and turned toward the wall. They dropped sickeningly into the moon, story after story in free fall, and then gradually the air brakes began to slow their descent. When they stepped out, the hallway seemed filled with girls, each with her Overone guard.

Then she was sitting with them all around her in the small auditorium; it amazed her how they resembled the girls in the lyceum.

An older brownrobe took the podium and microphone.

"As you know, it is the week for quarterly orientation. We have tested the pulsers and your responses; each of you has been timed. The slowest third will be redesigned. Carolyn Marris?"

A girl near the front stood up. She had curly blond hair and seemed no more than twelve.

"Come here."

She took the stage and stood, expressionless, beside the Overone.

"You were among the slowest to arrive. Was there some malfunction?"

"No, ma'am," she said in a military way.

"You came as rapidly as you could?"

"Yes, ma'am."

"As soon as you felt the pulser?"

"Yes, ma'am."

The Overone gave her audience a pleased smile. "Just as I thought," she said. "Design problem."

Slowly she turned and regarded the trembling girl.

"Report to Lab IV immediately," she said.

"Yes, ma'am."

Carolyn Marris walked from the stage, up the aisle past Saraj and out to her death.

The Overone consulted a list before her.

"Saraj Campbell?"

Saraj felt all the wrong things—rapid-fire pulse and tight jaws, icy, damp palms on the plastic armrests. Human feelings. She stood up rigidly and hurried to the stage.

"You were quick enough," the Overone said. "A much

more serious problem has arisen with you. What is your name, unit?'" she snapped.

"B10X13," Saraj replied instantly.

"What is Saraj Campbell?"

"Saraj Campbell is a temporary form of Overone service."

"Do you like this form?"

"B10X13 is indifferent to this question."

"Correct answer. Does Saraj like herself?"

"She is disposed toward positive responses."

"Excellent." The Overone addressed her group. "It would be a shame to commit this unit to total redesign. She has been assigned to a delicate mission and has performed it well until recently."

A streak of fear ran through Saraj's stomach.

"Unit B10X13, are you afraid to die?"

"B10X13 is indifferent to this question."

"Is she really? And is Saraj afraid?"

"Saraj is disposed—"

"Never mind that!" the Overone screamed. "What do you *feel*?!"

Saraj hesitated for an instant.

"I don't feel anything," she said sadly.

"That response carried a distinct emotional tonation."

"I am well designed."

The Overone looked shocked. "Answer when asked a question!" she yelled.

"Yes, ma'am."

"I think we are getting at the trouble," the Overone said through her microphone.

Saraj knew the probabilities. There was almost no chance to escape the factory now. Some units were brought back with altered programming, but looking nearly the same. And sometimes their new memories overlapped the old. But more often they went back to organic raw material, cryogenic suspension, spare parts.

"What is the most serious infraction a unit can commit?" the Overone asked.

"An action tending to reveal our natures," Saraj replied.

"Correct. Now, this evening you knew that a humanoid was leaving your dormpound — totally unauthorized — and possibly acting in concert with others in an unknown scheme."

"Yes, ma'am."

"Explanation?"

"My instructions called for me to make field decisions of this kind."

"*Field* decisions?!" the Overone cried. "Is that what you choose to call it?"

"My programming is specific."

"So it's *our* fault you allowed this to happened?"

"No, ma'am."

"Clarify."

"If I reported the humanoid's disappearance, my cover would have been exposed and my usefulness ended."

The Overone looked out at her audience. "This sounds to me like a programming defect. You," she said to Saraj, "you could justify anything in the name of your cover, couldn't you?"

"No, ma'am."

"That will be all. It's a shame — you were a fine unit in many ways — but we can certainly do better. Lab III is ready for you. Report at once."

Saraj left the stage and walked slowly up the aisle.

The clear eyes of the girls followed her as she went, expressing what anyone would have called compassion.

8

THE INJECTION

Tamara's fingernails dug into her brother's arm.

"He's dead," she whispered.

"Not yet I'm not."

It was his deep voice from the darkness.

"*Father*!?"

"Up here."

He slid down from the rocks above the cave.

"They missed me. I think they killed Bjorn, though."

Drewyn was beside his father now. "They did. We flew over them." He looked toward the ruins of his father's home. "What about your manuscripts? And all your notes?"

"Gone."

"Oh, Father."

"It doesn't matter. I've been fooling myself, thinking there was a way to publish my last book. This has brought me out of the daydream."

"Is your lab gone, too?" Tamara asked.

"I saved a few things — I'll tell you about that. Where's Jaric?"

"Arrested. They monitored his transmission to Tamara. She's had a mental picture of him in Central . . . on the table, wired."

Ryland was shocked for a moment and then sadness came into his blue eyes.

"It had to happen sometime." He reached for his daughter's hand. "Tamara, you're our best hope to save him."

"I am? Why?"

"Your remote vision. If you can hold your images a little longer and see the room clearly—how many Overones are with him, then—"

"But I can't control it that well!"

"Up until now."

"Father, we've got to do something *tonight*."

"Yes. I said I'd tell you what I saved from the lab. You know I've been working for years on the genetic basis of mental functions."

"Yes, sir."

"Well, for the past six months I've concentrated on DNA patterns of telepathic animals. Most of my research has been using the historical diskettes Drewyn lifted from the main library. It's fortunate the Overones don't care about such—"

"Father," Drewyn said gently.

"Of course. The short of it is, Tamara, I can give you an injection, and it will dramatically increase your telepathic abilities, including remote vision. With your permission, that is."

She stood in the sandust feeling the chilly breeze and taking it in.

"I don't know enough about this, naturally. And it might take time for you to adjust, but—"

"Let's do it," she said. "Do it right now."

She was surprised when he took the small bundle from beneath his left arm and began to unroll it on the sand. He had a bottle of fluid and a syringe, and he quickly drew the liquid up through it. "I thought we'd need to do this for another purpose," he said. "Tell you about it later. . . ."

Tamara hated shots and she was queasy watching, so she closed her eyes and breathed deeply.

It hurt and she teared up; then it was done.

"No point in trying Drewyn," her father said. "His telepathy was never as strong as yours."

She sat down in the cool sand and crossed her arms as the swirling began. There were light streaks across her private black sky. *I'm changing*, she thought. *I'm changing right now.*

"Think about Jaric," her father's voice said. He seemed far off, from another time. *Jaric. Yes. Sweet Jaric.*

"No!" she said, seeing him on the Table of Truth. "He looks awful!"

"Tamara," her father said, "keep him in view. Keep him steady, understand?"

She nodded.

"Is he on the table?"

"Yes."

"Is he alive?"

"Yes, sir."

"Good. Now, very slowly, I want you to move your eyes to the right. Past Jaric on around the room. Are you doing that?"

"Yes, sir," she said in a trance voice.

"Do you see anyone else?"

"Overones."

"Count them. Count them carefully, slowly."

"Three."

"Good. Are you seeing past them? To the wall?"

"Yes."

"Then come back, slowly. Come to Jaric again."

"I have him. Oh, Father!"

"Shhhhh. Calm now. Breathe."

In a moment she nodded, her eyes still closed.

"Look to the left. See anybody else?"

"One. That's all."

"All right. Now, Tamara, I want you to pull back from the table, ease away, as if you were backing through a door."

"Okay."

"Good. Keep going, keep going. You're passing through the wall. Keep on. Out into another space. Do you see it?"

"Yes."

"What's it like?"

"Just a hallway. Nobody's here."

Then Tamara spun away from the scene, around in a whirling, sickening spiral, seeing sparklers on a black summer night or nebulae sliding on the velvet of space.

"I can't hold it," she said, sinking to her knees. "Something's wrong with me."

Her father knelt and hugged her. "You did fine. At least we know he's still in there. Maybe you'll pick up something else on the way."

They climbed aboard the little ship again, this time with Tamara half collapsed in her father's lap. "I hate rushing this drug," he said. "But it seems to have worked. You may be sick for a few days, Tamara. I injected a bear once—"

"You what!" Drewyn said.

"One of the desert bears. I tried an experiment to make him telepathic . . . wanted to see what it would do to their survival, and whether it would lead to any kind of culture."

"What happened?" Tamara asked weakly.

"Oh, most interesting! He began to know when the hunters were coming and to lead the others away. Caused a real stir among the Overones. They finally got him with a big drive. Used light cruisers, long lines of men, laser guns . . ."

"We'll be at the lockbay for Central Research in two minutes," Drewyn said.

"Right. Now listen, kids. We're going to get him out of there, and then we'll steal a space vessel and take off for Old Earth."

"*Earth*!" they said together.

"There's no place left for us here, is there? I knew they'd come for me soon, when the bears were gone — they'll want that hunting station for something else now, and that was the last really secure airsource for me. Besides, now they're onto you and Jaric — no telling what they've taken from his brain."

"We've talked about going to earth . . ." Drewyn said slowly.

"But the position of the moon has to be right," Tamara said.

"It's close enough right now. I've worked out the plan in every detail, you know that."

"I never really thought we'd use it," Tamara said.

"Me, either," Drewyn added. "I guess it's all that propaganda about life on earth being extinct . . . and the death clouds . . . it scares you to think about."

"Don't believe it," Ryland said. "I've been taking sightings, and I've come to believe earth's environment could still be very tenable. Maybe even — "

"What?" Tamara asked. "You were going to say, 'Maybe Mother — ?' Could she be alive?"

"It's possible," her father said. He had more spirit in

his voice than she'd heard in a long time. "Want to find out?"

"Sure," she smiled. In a few seconds her future had been taken away from her, and a new one created.

"One minute," Drewyn told them.

"Okay, listen," Ryland said. "Drewyn, get us past the lockbay and fly right to the landing pad on Central."

"Yes, sir."

"Let me out, and you take off again. Stay beneath the domesky; fly fast—random patterns—and be back at that pad in exactly ten minutes."

"You're going in by yourself?"

"That's right. Now listen, at nine and a half minutes, make a pass by the far end of the building and blast out a window or create the best diversion you can think of. Got that?"

"Yes, sir."

"Good. Jaric and I will either be out there, or we won't— no second chances. If we're not in sight, head for the Arth Mountains. You know the plan."

"How are you going to get him out?"

"I've got an old laser pistol, son. It'll be enough for a few of these bureaucrats in Central."

"That's not what they are," Tamara said, her eyes closed. "I see them clearly and they . . . something's wrong, it's horrible! Father, I see them, they're taking Jaric off the table and . . ."

"Here comes the lockbay. Make it fast."

"Two of them don't have faces!"

"Robotic," he said calmly.

"But they move so well!"

"Organic. The moon's full of them now, Tamara."

"They're shaking Jaric!" she cried. "They're jerking him back and forth!"

"Hush now," Drewyn said. "They could sensor us as we pass through the gates."

The ship slowed and came to a hover.

Drewyn punched up his mailcode and the outerlock grid slowly divided. It opened like a mouth to take them.

9

THE MEASURE OF TRUTH

Saraj walked out of the auditorium and down the long corridor. Another thirty seconds and she would be in the laboratory section. *Will they do it quickly?* she wondered. She had heard once of a unit whose consciousness was kept alive in suspension—to let her think over the mistakes she had made. But perhaps it was just a story. *Part of Overstory*, she thought bitterly.

Lab III—there it was.

Just for an instant she imagined running. But to where? She really had no friends except Tamara and Drewyn who were her assignment, her problems. And they were human, of course, and knew nothing of Saraj's identity—*An identity they can take away with a switch or change as they wish*, she thought. Her palm slid up and down on the cold metal panel of the door, hesitating; then she pushed it open. "Come in!" a tall Overone declared. She was obviously excited about her task, and she looked Saraj over almost solicitously.

"Unit B10X13, reporting as ordered," Saraj said.

"Cut the machine talk with me, kid," the Overone snapped. She brushed her hand on the lab table before her. "You're as human as the born-ones out there; you feel what they feel, you think in their little subject-object sentences . . . you do everything they do, and you do it better!"

Saraj, took a quick step backward.

The Overone smiled at this. "Reflexes like an animal!" she said proudly. "Wonder how I know so much?"

"Ah, yes, ma'am."

"Ha! Curious and truthful!"

The Overone suddenly bent over the tables as if in pain. She slammed her fist down on its padded surface three times. "Stupid!" she cried. "Stupid! Stupid! That's what they all are!" Saraj tried to guess what this was—some final test, no doubt, which could determine what form her redesign would take.

"I know so much because I *created* you, you beautiful child!" the Overone said. She rushed around the table and took Saraj's arms, squeezing them just below the elbows. "This is *my* lab! There are only five like you in all moonspace—and you're the first who's ever failed."

Saraj started to answer, but the Overone cut her short.

"I know! I know! I heard the so-called interview on the monitor! I read all the files! Do you think I haven't kept up with every single day you've lived?"

"Ah—"

"Don't answer! I know all the answers! It's *they* who should be redesigned! You did your duty, exactly as I would have done it in your place."

The Overone released Saraj and walked violently across the laboratory. Saraj noticed the scientific equipment along the walls and the recessed cryogenic storage vaults and reformation chambers. This was the strangest—and most human-acting, in a way—of all the Overones Saraj had ever met. She seemed to carry power around the room with her, and yet . . . she acted out the emotions that Saraj always wished she could express. Until this moment she hadn't realized Overones felt such things.

"Look at you!" the Overone cried as she hurried back to grab Saraj again. She buried her face in Saraj's neck for a moment. "Smell your skin! Look at the blue of your eyes, each one perfect! The auburn of your hair? I spent weeks on those details, *weeks!*"

Saraj was astonished. Only Tamara and Drewyn had ever said they cared for her. "But that was the least of it, the least," the Overone continued, hugging Saraj, who hugged her lightly in return. "I made you feel because *I* feel. You can fool your assignments because you really care for them! And that's only because *I* can care! You have *my* brain engrams, child!"

The Overone wept on Saraj's shoulder for what seemed a long time, then gently led her over to the padded table.

"Climb up here," she said softly.

Saraj's heartbeat rushed into her throat as she sat on the table and as she allowed the Overone to guide her into lying down.

"Inside this room," the Overone said calmly, "I am in charge—no one else. They can give me orders, certain choices . . . and then . . ."

She stepped to a wall switch and dimmed the lights.

"I am instructed, too, child. I cannot just let you walk out of here."

She affixed a soft plastic crown of electrode contacts to Saraj's head and began to attach them to her skin. She worked rapidly and skillfully, and only occasionally did it hurt. Finally, she stood behind Saraj's head, out of sight, and there was silence and waiting. What could she be doing next? Saraj listened to the faint electronic hum of a monitor. Her feelings ran back and forth in confusion; maybe this woman was on her side, somehow, and would let her live. But that last statement was too solemn, too full of sorrow. It occurred to Saraj that the whole question in the Overone's mind was a matter of her own needs — her possessiveness and pride in Saraj-as-her-product, and Saraj's own life-as-she-felt-it was of no concern. "Do not be frightened," the Overone said as she fastened the straps around Saraj's wrists and ankles.

Saraj was almost bold enough to make a crack to this woman, in hopes of confirming the strange bond she seemed to feel. But she was too well trained to try it.

"I have a new creation," the Overone said, raising her hands. Saraj looked up and saw the Overone cocking a small gun-device. She pressed it against Saraj's neck, and there was a mild snap and some pressure, but that was all. "It is something they tried for centuries to find on Old Earth. My staff like to call it my Electronic Truth Serum, but I prefer to think of it as the Measure of Truth. It's a thousand times more sensitive than what humanoids once called their "lie detector machine." When I designed you, I built in special receptors for truth-responses, and now at last I have the means to tap them with complete accuracy. Do you understand?"

"Yes." Saraj left off the obligatory "ma'am," to see whether the Overone would snap at her.

Instead, she stroked Saraj's thick, fine red hair.

And so Saraj knew; either this woman really cared for her, or she was far better at pretense than seemed possible.

"All right. Breathe deeply, my child, and answer my questions. First, are you loyal to your primary axioms of teaching?"

"Yes."

"And are you completely loyal to all corollaries of these, by whatever logical systems, or by any yet-undiscovered logic, as far as you know?"

"Yes."

"Very good. And was the problem discussed in your public interrogation simply a question of judgment? Were you merely protecting your cover, as you claimed?"

"Yes."

"You are telling the truth."

Saraj closed her eyes and waited. Of course she was being truthful. No one had asked her about her *feelings* for Tamara and Drewyn, only about her loyalty; and so far she hadn't brought the two together. That was a nice thing about being robotic, she thought. *I can separate parts of me for as long as I need to.* Saraj knew that Tamara and Drewyn couldn't do that.

"I have to modify you to some extent, Saraj." It was the first time the Overone had used her name. "What I'm going to do is replace a small right brain section; it's a center for connections between many of your integrated circuits—in fact," she laughed, "it's a rather mysterious area, because it's a place of interaction between the part of you that's electronic and the organic part. Even I don't know everything about it."

"What will happen?" Saraj asked.

"Ah, you question me now!"

"I only thought you wanted me to grasp—"

"Silence, child. Yes, yes, all right. It will give you loyalty chips with cleaner engraving, to put it very briefly. I don't think it will affect your memories, or your unit-identity, as they say, although I hate that word 'unit.'"

"I see."

The Overone came close to Saraj's face.

"Yes. This way I can tell them I've redesigned you. Act a little stiff around them at first."

"Yes."

"And one more thing, little one. I know you like the life I've given you; I can read fear in one of my children even without a digital fear-pain monitor. I know exactly what you want, and I'm giving it to you. But you'll owe me something in return."

"Yes?"

"Yes! Your absolute loyalty to Overstory! Don't fail me, now, on this mission. Go find out what your humanoid friend is up to and report as quickly as you can. There will be another mission waiting for you. This is what your life is for, Saraj; do you understand me?"

"Yes. Yes, ma'am."

"Good. Now you will lose your specific consciousness for a little while. This, too, might aid you later on, because you can know the thing humanoids fear most of all."

She waited until Saraj asked, "And that is?"

"That is death, my dear. You're going to experience it now."

10————————

COUNTDOWN

Drewyn flew away from Central as fast as he could.

"Why did I let him go in there alone?" Tamara said.

"What choice did you have?" He lifted them up so quickly that her head was pinned back against her seat rest.

"What are we going to do now? Just fly around for ten minutes?" she asked.

"Any better idea?"

He checked his instruments and listened to different frequencies—it didn't seem they were being followed.

"Oh, goodness!" Tamara cried.

"What is it?"

"Saraj! They'll drag _her_ into Central after we're gone."

"But she can't tell them anything, can she?"

"So what?" Tamara snapped. "When did that ever matter?"

"She doesn't even know about Father."

"No, nothing."

"Maybe they'll just scan her and let her go."

"Do you really believe that?" Tamara said.

"I guess not."

"Head for my dormpound."

"Wait a minute," Drewyn said. "You go back in there now, you're taking chances with Father and Jaric."

"We can't let Saraj be tortured for us, Drewyn."

"But how can you help things by talking to her? Won't that just make it worse in the scanning?"

"Just *do* it!" Tamara cried. "I'm not going to *talk* to her, for pity's sake! We're going to take her with us!"

Drewyn flew toward the dormpound without a word. This new idea made his heart race, because he had far stronger feelings for Saraj than he had ever admitted to anyone, even himself. *Take her with us. All the way to Old Earth. Yes*, he thought, giving the cruiser full throttle, *of course that's what we've got to do.*

"What if she doesn't want to come?" he suddenly asked.

"Well, I'm not going to *force* her!"

"All right, all right, calm down. We're three minutes from Father's drop-off, now." The dormpound appeared below them in the night. "It'll take you—what?—a minute to reach your room?"

"That's right."

"That's four. One with Saraj—five. Back up here at six. Three back to Central . . . that leaves one minute for our diversion."

"Okay, fine. If I'm not back in two minutes flat, leave without me."

"I'll *have* to."

"So, do it." She unlatched her cockpit door.

"Wait."

Drewyn reached under his seat and pulled out the laser pistol. "Take it and use it," he said. "Remember, you could kill every Overone in the dormpound, and it wouldn't make a difference now. If they catch us—"

"*Okay!*" she snapped, climbing from the cruiser.

She loped across the roof without another word.

Tamara's passage into the dormpound was as quick as she could make it, but she wished for earth-g as she hurried down the hall, praying for Saraj to be there.

The lights were out in their room, yet as she closed the door Tamara sensed her friend in the darkness.

"Saraj?"

"Shhhh. Don't turn it on, okay? I'm resting."

"Okay, *listen*. You're not going to believe me—oh, I don't mean that—it's—*look*, Saraj, I can't explain right now, but I'm in trouble and so are you."

"We are? Why?"

"I told you I don't have time to explain! I'm sorry, I didn't mean to yell. Listen. If you had fifteen seconds to decide whether to trust me and follow me to a new life . . . or to stay here and be scanned, maybe even tortured, because *they* think you know about me . . . could you decide?"

"Are you kidding, Tamara?"

"Ten seconds."

"I'd go with you."

"Where are your shoes?"

"On my feet—don't worry, I'm ready. Are we going up to the roof?"

"Yes—you know about that?"

"You better go first. I'll follow in just a—"

"No! Come now, or it'll be too late!'

"But if the Overones—"

"I've got a laser, Saraj. Now, come *on*."

"All right then, lead the way."

Tamara flung open the door and they loped. In exactly two minutes they were climbing into the light cruiser beside Drewyn. Saraj sat between them.

Then they were flying through the black sky toward Central Research.

Tamara tried to choose her words.

"My father is rescuing Jaric from the scanning area," she said. "If they make it out, we're picking them up, and we're going to steal a spacecraft and go to Old Earth. Can you take all that in?"

"Yes." She sounded too calm to Tamara, as if she were half asleep. "Really? I'm not sure *I* could, just like that!"

"Do you think we can live on Old Earth?" Saraj said almost dreamily. "You know they say it's poisonous now."

"It's a lie, Saraj. So much of what they teach us is lies. You'll see—Father will explain everything. Oh, I know this must be upsetting you, but if we hadn't *grabbed* you like this, they'd—"

"I'm not upset," she said in that same even, slightly distant voice. "You're in shock," Tamara said. "But never mind. Let's just get Father and Jaric right now."

They flew in silence for the last minute. Tamara couldn't shake the impression that Saraj was acting like somebody else.

As the lights of Central materialized in the distance, Drewyn spoke.

"I've got our diversion figured out, unless you've a better idea."

"What is it?" Tamara asked.

"We'll swing by another wing of the building and I'll open up with that laser pistol. Simple as that. Maybe we can start a fire."

"Fine."

Central was clear in outline now.

"Okay," Drewyn said, "get ready—hand me the laser when I say—stand by."

Tamara pulled it out and gave it to Saraj. "Here, you hold it," she said.

11 _____

A FATHER'S WISH

Ryland Langstrom loped down the hallway of Central with Jaric over his shoulder. Behind him, in the scanning room, five Overones sprawled dead; four of them were certainly robotic, from their facelessness, but the fifth seemed human. He had bled, but not much, and Ryland wondered if he was some new partly organic and partly electronic creation.

Jaric was unconscious and heavy. Ryland was a big man and he had kept in shape, but he couldn't carry this weight, even in moon-g, on a run for long; and his laser pistol was so hot he had to concentrate on keeping it away from his right leg.

He ducked into a recessed doorway to gasp for breath and listen.

In another minute his children ought to arrive, and he had to make the stairwell down the hall to reach the pad on the roof.

All right, he thought, *just do it now*. He ran, bent and huffing, fighting for breath, with his eyes on the stairs ahead. There were footsteps behind him and he simply pointed the laser backward and fired. Then he was climbing the steps and rounding the corner. The masonry shattered behind him as the Overones fired their silent laser rifles, much more powerful than his weapon.

He ran up, up . . . and the roof door came into sight, then he was pressing against it, his arm trembling as he tried the latch, holding the hot pistol . . . "Damn!" he cried, dropping it to open the door. Running boots were coming up the stairwell behind, and he slumped down with Jaric's limp body falling over him; he grabbed the laser and fired, sending the Overone down in a heap. Ryland dragged the young man by his armpits. He kept loping backward with the stubborn, resistant body, until he reached the protected enclave of the chimney corner. Then he propped Jaric up out of laser range and prepared to defend the roof.

When the doorway opened, three Overones popped out before he could take aim. They separated and fixed his position, then stood sighting their carbines. Ryland ducked, and a river of green fire passed over and around him, blasting the chimney top away. He flung them a return shot and then cowered against Jaric's body again. 'Uuhhhh," Jaric said. He began to work his dry lips. "*No! Don't come to now!*" Ryland said.

An Overone sailed into clear view, and Ryland took him out with an instinct shot. Then there was a terrible commotion of glassamyer shattering a block away, a series of windows breaking and breaking without end. Sirens went off and light cruisers with searchlights passed overhead. Ryland raised his eyes a few inches to see—this would be Drewyn and Tamara's diversion—then a flash lit up the world so brightly it seemed to be inside his body. He kept seeing it even through his squeezed-shut eyelids; it burned and burned right through his head, sending pain-rivers down his arms and chest. He clutched

at Jaric's moving body and tried to cry out but the rivers
were too hot for sound. "*Jaric!*" he screamed hoarsely,
"*Jaric, I'm hit! Don't move!*" Then he realized he was
blind.

Drewyn and Tamara and Saraj strafed Central with
the laser pistol and started two fires. They saw the flashes
of Ryland's battle and were starting there when patrol
cruisers arced high overhead and crossed them with
searchlights. Drewyn flew low, drawing them, and then
he cut his lights and shot through a ground-level walkway
beneath a second-floor enclosure. The two ships collided
with each other and exploded behind him.

In a few seconds he was over his father on the roof
pad, and he saw the Overones jump back into the stairwell at his ship's approach. They fired at him, and he
knew from the flashes that they had laser rifles and that a
single contact could bring him down. He flew to the
building's far side, putting his father in the middle, and
hovered just below roof level.

"Let me out!" Saraj commanded. "I'll get them for
us!"

"You're not strong enough," Drewyn said, trying to
think.

She took the ball on the end of his pilot's stick and
crushed it with one hand. "Let me out," she said again.
This time he hit the cockpit cover release. She stood on
the seat back and leapt, and they saw her rise and disappear slowly over the edge.

"Good grief!" Drewyn said. "How could she—?"

"I don't know, but she can't get them out alone,"
Tamara said, rising on her seat. "Lift us just a little."

Drewyn eased the ship upward, and as the roof came

into reach Tamara jumped for it, hung struggling on the edge for a moment and then scrambled over and rolled.

Saraj was running toward her with Jaric over her back. She laid him down on the ledge and cried, "Get him aboard!"

Then she was gone again. Jaric was groaning and trying to move, groping to wake up, it seemed, thrashing in slow motion. She and Drewyn got him into the little ship.

Then an Overone fired at them and the light-stream shattered their raised cockpit lid. Tamara scrambled aboard as Drewyn dropped down two stories and accelerated, then came up in a fast, wide loop to pass over the roof again. But now it was crowded with Overones firing laser rifles and manning searchlights, and in the night sky there were the lights of a police cruiser formation coming straight at them. "We've got to go!" Drewyn screamed.

"There they are!" Tamara said. "She's carrying him, too!"

"Where?!" he yelled, forcing the ship into a tight circle. The light-fire rose in straight columns all around them.

"There! But she's going the wrong way!"

Drewyn cut his lights and flew at full speed away from the police squadron.

"Oh, Drewyn! She was bringing him right through them, in the midst of them, and they made way for her! Why?"

Drewyn skimmed the buildings so closely that the police unit flying behind him slowed up.

Now Saraj was on the roof's edge waving desperately; their father lay at her feet. For no reason Tamara and Drewyn could see, the Overones were all loping away.

Drewyn maneuvered to just below the ledge, and Saraj bent over to lift Ryland again. But the guards reappeared, blasting green light, and a stream hit Saraj in the shoulder and sent her over into the open cockpit on top of Tamara.

Drewyn shot away in the little ship, then circled for another approach, but now the roof was covered with the firing robots, and Tamara saw two of them dragging her father into the stairwell that led below.

"*They've got him*!" she screamed from beneath Saraj's motionless body. "I saw them take him away!"

Jaric groaned and stirred beside her.

Drewyn heard the police radio calling for interception and backup.

He turned and flew toward the Arth Mountains, as his father had said he should. There would be time to think — and to grieve — later, but not now.

"*What are you doing*?!" Tamara screamed. "*I don't want to go without him! Make another attack!*"

"Suicide," Drewyn said. "We'll be lucky to get away at all now. And if we can make it to Old Earth, you know that's what he'd want us to do."

"Want us to do? What does that have to do with it?!"

But she couldn't stop him; he wouldn't even answer her. She would have grabbed the controls from him if she'd known how, and if Saraj hadn't been sprawled helpless across her body.

"We can't leave him, Drewyn," she said in a pitiful voice. "You know we can't."

But her brother was flying hard, thinking only of escape.

12 ⸻

SILENT PASSAGE

Drewyn skimmed low across the plains. In a few moments the sharp curve of the moon's empty horizon gave way to the steep foothills and then the sheer cliffs of the Arth Mountains, where iron and cinnabar strip mining would be in full operation day or night. No ship seemed to be following them, but Drewyn assumed there would be an ambush somewhere ahead. Still, if it didn't come soon they might just get away; Ryland had worked out this plan over many years. The first step was to hide the little rocket cruiser, and Drewyn knew the exact spot his father had chosen.

He slowed and then made a gentle landing in the deep, black shadow of an abandoned iron pit that lay between two well-lit and active mine craters. He brought the cruiser to rest beside the sheer rock wall where an old, wrecked pressure door hung awkwardly on its hinges. In a few moments they had the cave room open and the cruiser jammed inside; then they replaced the door and began brushing away their landing marks in the soft moondust with a broom Ryland had ready for them.

Without a word they took up their burdens, Drewyn carrying Jaric, who by now was moaning and thrashing, fighting his way back to consciousness, and Tamara carrying the limp form of Saraj over her shoulder. The task wasn't too difficult, except for Jaric's wild swings, and they first made their way along the tops of small meteoroids to avoid footprints, and then they began loping in great, soft bounds across the ink-black space, guided only by the star-pattern above that Ryland had identified and prepared them for. Thus they navigated to the center of the old mine cut, and here they flashed their spotlight for just long enough to locate the levitation belt.

The next step was to dig out the small magnicar that Ryland had buried in the deep dust and marked with a triangle of rocks. Jaric was really coming to now, and he sat down and held his head as they worked. Soon they had freed the four-seater from the surface, lifted it onto the magnetic track and climbed aboard with Saraj and Jaric. Drewyn hit the switch to pressurize the cockpit, and when the meter read SAFE they took off their helmets.

"How are you feeling?" Drewyn asked Jaric.

"Eghh."

"At least you're here."

"Where's Ryland?"

"He didn't make it."

Tamara turned her head away and said nothing.

"Saraj? She came too?" Jaric asked.

"Yeah," Drewyn said. "And she's hit. Listen. We all know the plan. We'll just have to carry Saraj and pretend she's sick, if we have to."

Jaric closed his eyes and held his temples. "I don't know what's wrong with me," he said.

"You were under brainscan," Tamara said. "No telling what else."

"Well, let's get going," he said, irritably. "It won't help me if we're caught again."

Tamara thought this was the oddest tone she'd ever heard from Jaric. He was always so warm and charming; they must have really worked him over in Central. *Well, he'll come back with a little time*, she thought. She turned to Saraj, who lay back against her seat with her mouth open, barely breathing. "Hang on, Saraj," she whispered.

Drewyn started the magnicar and they began to move. The sensation was gentle, and they gradually picked up speed, were pressed back against their cushioned seats and soon reached a hundred miles an hour flying effortlessly over the magnetic field of the track.

Now they were just one more magnicar among the thousands of others on the levitation belt grids of the lunar surface.

They traveled on and on, taking a few diversionary by-paths, working their way toward Launchfield Station III. There were five launch sectors now, with giant levitation tracks of many different designs and lengths, to take care of the endless variety of spacecraft. Ryland had watched the guards and technicians as they processed the lifts, and he had worked out the best chance. They wouldn't try to steal a small, compact unit; this is what the Overones would search for first. They wouldn't take a rocket vehicle, loaded with its vast weight of liquid fuel for an earth-return. There weren't many of these giants left, anyway, and they were too easy to explode with a laser strike, or just by the accidents caused by untried hands. No, they would steal a huge factory ship, a great cylinder the size of an ocean liner on Old Earth. And Ryland had studied the lineup on Launchfield III until he'd picked out the perfect vessel: the *Tomorrow*, a class ten manufacturing

craft, outfitted for biological work but awaiting assignment until all its instruments could undergo their five-
year inspection. Ryland had joked with Drewyn about its
name—maybe a lucky one, he had said, bringing them all
a new beginning.

Drewyn piloted them to within a hundred yards of the
spacecraft. Then he and the others put their pressure
helmets back on, climbed out and lifted the magnicar
from its track. They left it there.

Slowly, normally, they loped across the launchway to
the ship, Drewyn leading, Jaric and Tamara carrying
Saraj between them. There was not even a single guard,
and in a short time the four of them were inside the pressurized control module. They slipped off their helmets
again, strapped themselves into their seats and Drewyn
prepared to launch.

"You were going to be our captain," he said to Jaric,
smiling, "but I think I'd better do it."

"Suit yourself," Jaric said, glaring out the spaceport at
the brilliant sky. Tamara, sitting behind him, reached
forward to touch his neck, just to comfort him, but
something made her draw back. He was so cold—the
Overones had really done something to him, with drugs
or electricity—something.

Then they were moving.

Ahead, the long ribbon of levitation track glimmered
in starlight as they picked up speed, went faster and
faster, then flew without even the friction of air, cradled
in their shaped magnetic field. They covered the sixty
miles of the launch track in less than a minute and were
flung without the slightest vibration into space. They had
surpassed escape velocity for the moon—5,200 mph—
and now they floated free. Drewyn fired the small vernier

rockets to swing the ship around the edge of the moon, and they saw the blue earth floating in the black sky before them. Drewyn locked it into the ship's automatic-pilot computer function, cut the engines, and they were on their way. They wouldn't need another bit of power, not even a drop of fuel, because already they were riding a long arc of centrifugal force out from the moon's equator, destined on this course to graze earth's upper atmosphere in three days; then, captured by gravity, they would float into stationary orbit there. It was a beautiful plan, a masterpiece of simplicity. Ryland would be proud of them if he knew.

"Let's see what we can do for Saraj," Tamara said.

"All right," Jaric mumbled. "But we're weightless now, remember? Just stay in your seat and let me check her."

"Go ahead," Tamara said as agreeably as she could. She was more than ready for the real Jaric to come back.

He unstrapped his suit and floated up to the top of the craft. They all smiled for the first time as they waited for him to work with it. "It's so much harder than moon-g!" he cried. Then he pushed off with his boots, floated down to Saraj's seat and grabbed its arm. Slowly, he pulled back the torn S-suit where the Overone's laser had struck her. "Wait a minute," he said. "*Wait a minute!*"

"What is it, Jaric?" Drewyn asked.

"*Wires!*" he yelled. "She's got *circuitry* inside her wound!"

"That's not possible," Tamara said as she unbelted.

"She's not *human!*" Jaric cried. "She's a robot—the best one I ever saw. You come look. Drewyn, your little girl friend is a machine!" Angrily, he turned loose of the chair and drifted into the ship's space again, just as Tamara was kicking off the ceiling and diving for Saraj.

Drewyn's stomach was doing flips. *How had Jaric known his feelings for Saraj? And what did he mean — wires?*

"Did you hear me, Drewyn?" Jaric said, now floating over his head.

"Take the controls," Drewyn said.

"Sure," Jaric snapped. "See for yourself. Tamara's best friend! Hey, Tamara? Did the Overones think you were so smart they'd spy on you with a robot?"

"Shut up, Jaric," she said quietly.

"Hey! You two think we're escaping? They'll have homing devices all over that thing! They're just letting us get far enough out so we won't hurt a station, then they'll blast us right out of spacesky."

"Let me tell you something, Jaric," Drewyn said in a controlled voice. "Just now I was punching in the bio codes for Lab Base. Remember when Father showed us how to do that?"

"Sure do. You still think there's a point?"

"If he was right, our computer will transmit three days' worth of data, and it's good enough to make them believe we're an official mission."

"Don't tell me, Drewyn! I was there! Did you hear what I just said about Saraj?"

"Easy, Jaric. You'll see on the screen where I was. Why don't you carry out the coding operation, and let us worry about Saraj."

"Sure thing, partner. But if that thing comes to, you better watch out."

Drewyn unstrapped Saraj and gently removed her helmet. She was the same pale color, hardly breathing, and she seemed neither asleep nor comotose, but rather preserved in some way.

"Oh, no," Drewyn said softly. "Just look."

"Infection," Tamara said.

"What are we going to do now?" Drewyn asked. "Jaric, can you check the ship's medical files for a case like this?"

"I wasn't going to," Jaric said.

He was reaching into a storage locker, and when he turned he held their laser pistol.

"And what does that mean?" Drewyn asked.

"It means there are more important things to do, Drewyn. You can spend time with the med files if you want to, but I've got to concentrate on saving all of us."

"Oh, sure," Drewyn said angrily, "except that you happen to be the one who knows all the access codes."

"Look," Jaric said, "even if we do manage to bring Saraj back now, what is she? I mean, *what is she*?"

"She's our friend, Jaric, that's who she is."

"And maybe not. Maybe she's nobody's friend, because she's a *thing*. A *thing*, Drewyn. Have you been thinking about that?"

Drewyn floated, trembling, searching for the perfect words to put a cold stop to Jaric. He needed time to deal with this himself. But if Saraj could just come back to them, just come back and be all right again, surely she'd prove herself.

"I'll tell you what you do," Drewyn said at last. "You worry about fooling the Overones if they contact us, and you leave Saraj to me."

"Fine," Jaric said. "That's what I had in mind to begin with."

He turned back to the window, the pistol in his lap, and stared out into the bright, starry sky. *It makes no sense*, he thought. *It's as if I've come to in a crazy world.*

And I can't seem to wake up all the way. Each sound they make is so irritating.

Drewyn hovered with his sister over Saraj. He was too shaken to say anything, and she touched his arm in comfort. They stared at the red and swollen wound.

"We don't know what to do," Drewyn said bitterly. "And if she's not . . . if she's not *all* human, we don't know how to treat her."

"It won't be in the files, either," Tamara said.

"No."

"Let me try something," she said.

Tamara held herself close beside Saraj and breathed deeply and slowly. She calmed her mind, first by rolling her eyes back twenty degrees to induce alpha brainwaves; then she closed her eyes and focused on Saraj's wound. The image was steady before her, and she simply held it there, letting herself become almost blank, almost asleep.

She saw beneath the puffed, inflamed surface of Saraj's skin, and there was a fibrous network of blood vessels intermingled with a mass of filament circuitry. Deeper and deeper Tamara penetrated, exploring the healthy tissue and absorbing its strange texture. It was neither animal flesh nor electronic maze, but some blend of these two. Tamara's discipline allowed her to think about this new tissue slowly, without breaking her trance. When she was gazing at it calmly, examining its threads — one carrying a pulse of blood, another twisted about, transmitting a flash of electric energy — she asked herself how to heal the infected path of the laser's burn.

Clearly, as in a slow-motion dream, she saw her own hands over the wound; they were almost touching it, and they felt very warm and then hot. She opened her eyes and lightly touched her fingertips together, and the dream-heat became real. She extended her joined hands over Saraj's wound, and a rhythm of energy began, very gently, to flow out of her in steady waves. Her hands and then her arms became hotter, and she closed her eyes and rested her consciousness on the single image of the swollen wound. Just below her right collarbone, exactly where Saraj was hurt, Tamara felt a sharp bite of pain. The heat flooded her now, and the pain ran straight into her like a rough spike. The energy waves grew faster in their pattern, and her hands felt close to catching fire. At once the pain-spike exploded inside her shoulder and she floated upward grabbing for it, rolling over slowly in weakness and chill, icy coldness running into her from wet, numb hands. She could see only blackness before her as she rolled, and her shoulder was an island of heat in the frozen darkness of her body. The spike was alive inside her, a rigid, invisible shaft shot with electricity, but it was a hot animal invader, too, a snake—*yes*, Tamara thought as she twisted over and over in the free space of the ship, knocking Drewyn aside and clutching herself as she rolled—*it's a snake in my shoulder, looking to turn and blow up.* Then she bounced off the wall with her head, and the burning snake was gone, and her brother was holding her, and the lights came back, too bright to face.

"Tamara?" a scratchy, unused female voice said.

They looked down and Saraj was smiling up at them.

13

BLUE EARTH RISING

Within a few minutes Saraj seemed strong again, and they told her what had happened since she'd been shot. Jaric remained sullen at the controls, with his back to them, and they found it more comfortable to move to the very rear of the command module, and to whisper.

Saraj smiled at the way Drewyn kept staring at her. Then she became glum and said, "You don't know whether you . . . even care for me now, do you?"

"Of course I do!" he said, embarrassed.

But then neither of them knew what to say.

Tamara decided to leave them alone for a while. She got some dried soybeans and powered orange juice, mixed them with water and brought the food up to sit beside Jaric. When she was strapped in, she handed his cups to him.

"Thanks," he said.

Her heart jumped at this small hint of kindness. But he didn't meet her eyes.

"Jaric," she said slowly, "are you aware that you aren't yourself? Since the brainscan they did on you?"

"I feel lousy, Tamara. How would you feel?"

"The same way, I'm sure. Look, I'm sorry. I won't keep bothering you."

"Good."

She looked out the windows on her side. *All right, let him be a grouch for now; surely it will pass*, she thought. She closed her eyes and concentrated on her father. For just a moment she saw him in a cell, sitting on the floor, with bandages around his hands and eyes. Father! *But at least he's alive, and he's not being tortured.*

Out in the blackness of space, the earth was already larger, clear and blue against the nothingness. Tamara began to think about what awaited them. Ryland had believed there was still life there, but probably in a wild and primitive condition. The strangest thing of all would be constant earth gravity . . . she would never again have the freedom of moon-g, only one sixth that of earth! It would mean more work for her heart, and a shorter life . . . eighty or ninety years at best . . . so she was giving up the last forty with this one three-day trip. And the other amazing change would be twelve-hour days, after living so many years, her whole life, with day and night seasons that were each three hundred fifty-four hours, twenty-two minutes, and one second long!

She'd be able to walk about under the natural, gravity-captured sky, breathing freely without the weight of liquid oxygen tanks on her back and without a pressurized helmet. Also, Ryland said the sunlight would feel warm and pleasant—unlike the 240-degree surface temperatures on Luna, with steady, burning rays that would roast you in a minute without your aluminized skin-suit. Maybe the most fun would be during the nights, without minus-260-degree freezes, and with the oddest sight of all, the little real moon, hanging in the Old Earth sky.

"Are you looking forward to it?" she tentatively asked Jaric.

He breathed a long, slow sigh. "Here's how I see it,

Tamara. No more flying, no Spaceforce training. No future except turning into a savage, maybe, at the best. There could be a lot of mutants down there, you know, monsters, for all we can imagine."

"And we might find Mother, too."

He glanced at her once and squinted. "Sure, Tamara. Sure we will."

She unstrapped and floated black to Drewyn and Saraj, who were sitting very close together in the rear of the compartment. They were watching the growing earth-planet out their spaceport, and they smiled warmly at Tamara. In spite of Ryland's capture, in spite of Jaric's surprising meanness, they couldn't help feeling excited about the prospect before them. And Tamara, holding out her arms to them and grinning, couldn't either.

The three days passed more quickly than Tamara would have thought, and there was no attempt to contact them by radio, no spacecraft came in pursuit and no shots from the giant solar-mirrors were fired. It seemed their escape had been perfect, though such good luck was too much to trust. Finally, above a spectacular red dusk spread below them in the atmosphere, they docked their massive bio-ship at one of the old colonies.

"Now comes the tricky part," Drewyn said as he assumed the copilot's position. "These industrial freighters were never meant to penetrate the atmosphere of a planet. After docking like this, in the old days, passengers and cargo would travel between here and the surface by means of a winged aircraft."

"I know," Tamara said. "It was called the shuttle."

"Yes," he smiled. His spirit was exuberant. "And there's just a chance that one is still parked up here in the holding bay."

"Surely not with fuel," Tamara said.

"It's possible. Father says everyone left Old Earth in such a hurry at the end of the last war . . . anything's possible."

Jaric put on his skin-suit and his pressurized helmet, sharply refusing any assistance or company, and went through the bay doors into the lab section of the *Tomorrow*. From there he entered free space, anchored only by a long, thin tethercord, and worked his way to the holding compartment of the space station.

It was empty. A shuttle had been too much to hope for.

Back inside the command module he gave them the news. "Well, Plan B," he said. "We'll have to fly this thing down." He looked around at its walls. "Ryland didn't want us to use it unless we had to, because of the exhaust pollution, but we have no choice. I'm for getting this over with. Okay?"

"Yeah, okay with me," Drewyn said, looking at the others.

They agreed.

"How are you planning to plot a course?" Saraj asked Jaric.

"Don't *you* worry about it, machine."

"Jaric!" Drewyn and Tamara cried together.

"All right, all right." He turned and strapped himself into his pilot's chair. Saraj moved close to Drewyn and whispered coordinates to him.

"They'll take us down about a hundred miles south of your mother, near a big lake system," she said. "It'll be our best chance for a soft landing."

He looked shocked, but she only cautioned, "Shhhh."

Then he acted as casually as he could and passed this on to Jaric, pretending it was information from Ryland.

"I don't know . . ." Jaric said. "Landing on a lake? That sounds risky. Why didn't Ryland tell me about it?"

Drewyn shrugged. "He wasn't thinking we'd go so soon, remember?"

"Yeah. But how did he know where Tava would be?"

"It's a place they talked about . . . before her escape."

"Well. Let's try it, then."

Are they holding back information from me? Jaric wondered. *Nothing feels right. I can't trust any of them. And their voices sound so raw.*

They passed all the way around the globe during the earth-night period, seeing the blinding sun beside the black-velvet space sky for the last time.

Then, a little before dawn at their target location, they disengaged from the station and fired the fusion engines. They wouldn't need a great deal of power to control the descent, and fortunately the stream of radioactive moon-dust exiting the ship would be small. The design of the *Tomorrow*, a long cylinder, wasn't bad for resisting the burning air friction on their way down, and the only shame was that it would be making its last flight. The space vessel was not made for ascent through an atmosphere; its engines could never achieve anything like the 25,000 mph escape velocity necessary on Old Earth.

So they angled down in a peach-and-gray-streaked sky, faster and faster in the long descending curve the ship's computer had plotted. When they reached the danger point of friction heat, Jaric reversed the ship and put the engines on auto, and let the computer slow their final flight.

Then, in the distance of the great horizon, they saw the lake system shining silver in the early light. The lakes shone like metal skins, and for a single moment of panic they all wondered whether Jaric could do it. He hit the manual override switch and eased the ship forward ever so slightly, increased the reverse thrusters and, like a great impossible balloon, the *Tomorrow* came downward, downward, skimming over the faces of a trillion little bright waves, touching the tops of them, planing then across the wide, sun-bright surface, dipping down and churning slower and slower now like a giant ship lost from the sea and foundering on this tiny window-opening of life. They slid and churned into endless shallows, slicing over miles of cattails in bubbling mud, the engines cut now, only momentum carrying them against the friction of swamp bottom and reed beds, and suddenly, at last, they came to rest beside a bank of thick pine trees.

14

WHO IS THIS AMONG US?

The ship lay half buried in swamp marsh. It life-support systems still functioned, and its computer screen blinked silently, alive. Tamara felt sick as she slowly unstrapped from her astronaut's chair.

"Red light," her brother said softly, looking out at the sky.

"Daybreak," Jaric said. "Our first dawn on our own planet."

Tamara hurried to the spaceport that was now above them. It was filled with clear, red sunlight.

"Real sky," she said, smiling, feeling better with excitement. "It's our *home*! Let's get the door open!"

"Wait, hold on," Jaric said. "You know how often your father spoke about death gases on Old Earth."

"Yes, he did. But how can we tell?" Drewyn asked.

"I'll search the computer banks. Since they were programmed with an earth-landing possibility, there must be a detection system."

Tamara touched the inner surface of the window. Through that perfectly transparent glassamyer was the real sky and the old wind of her father's stories. Suddenly a hummingbird appeared before her, suspended in the air.

"Look!" she cried. "We don't need the ship's computer!"

Jaric and Drewyn came up on either side of her, and the little green hummingbird moved a few inches, hovered and then vanished.

"I guess you're right," Jaric said.

"Let's open the door then!" Tamara cried.

"But listen, the winds can kill you here—remember that. The air can be fine, and before you know it, poisonous clouds or radiation fog can roll in on you. So let's go slow."

"I don't see any clouds," Tamara said.

"All right, all right," Jaric grumbled.

He unlatched the door around the porthole and punched the opening series on the wall panel. Slowly, without a sound, as if in invitation, the door eased outward.

"I'll go first!" Tamara said.

"All right," Jaric said, "but have a quick glance—that's it—don't let more than your head out of the ship yet."

Thinking he was being foolish, Tamara looked around for something to stand on, and Drewyn offered his interlocked hands. She fitted her left foot there, seized the edges of the opening, and he raised her up.

She caught her breath at the sight. There were thick, spreading pines, far bigger than any on the garden islands encircling the moon or grown beneath the airdomes, and they seemed knotted together by tight tangles of dark vines and brush. But they were a little way off, and between the ship and the woods lay a flat of water and mud and tall, waving grasses. Redwing blackbirds floated back and forth on weak reeds. "Oh!" Tamara said, "they're just like in the books!"

"What are?" Jaric asked, irritated. "Come on—we want to see, too."

They all climbed out and walked along the slick side of the fat, overturned ship. When they reached the point nearest the trees, Tamara said, "I'm not afraid!" as she jumped feet first off into the marsh. Water splashed up on them as she sunk down to her knees, laughing, and then she sucked her feet free of the mire and began to walk. After twenty yards of only sinking to her ankles, she turned and beckoned the others.

Rather than jump, they carefully slid down the ship's side, bristled at the chilly water and followed her. Soon they climbed up the bank of yellow clay and entered the sweet darkness of the forest.

"It's wonderful!" Tamara cried, feeling the rough vines and wild, waxy leaves of unknown plants. "It smells better than the greenhouse!"

"Yes," Drewyn agreed. For an instant they glanced at Saraj, wondering if she could actually smell; but they didn't want to ask.

"This is something," even Jaric admitted, shaking his head slowly as he stared into the mysterious, thickety trees.

They walked on through for half a mile, unable to stop the exploring urge. They had no plan and no food, and they'd left their ship's door open, but nobody could stop walking in his wild forest where no Overone had ever stepped.

When they came to the bright light and the open meadow on the far side of the pines, they stood just inside the shadows to watch. Wind — far stronger than any in the airdomes — swept over the sage in graceful bursts and strokes, shimmering the grass-heads in patterns of morning light. Then they saw the deer. There were at least twenty on the far side of the meadow, grazing along the edge of low, twisted trees.

The four all stood in silence, awed by the majesty and silence of this new world, wondering why their ancestors had chosen to destroy it for themselves.

Suddenly the deer all turned and ran down the row of trees to their left, white tails flying high. Behind them, not far up the slope, other animals were racing after them.

"What are they?" Drewyn said in alarm.

"Wolves!" Tamara said. "Jaric, did you bring the laser?"

"No! Let's get back, now!"

They all turned to run, and Tamara felt the breeze across their backs as they disappeared into the trees and realized it was blowing directly from the wolves. She knew from books that wolves had amazing noses.

They kept up a steady pace, but it was hard to remember just how they'd come before, and the vines seemed to reach out for them. In a few moments they were sweating and tearing through briars their tongues dry and hot inside their mouths. There had been so many wolves—if that's what they were—and they ran so fast!

Finally the low clay bluff over the great, unbroken marsh appeared, and they jumped off, one by one, into the water. They slogged ahead as best they could, waiting on no leader, and Jaric was first to reach the high and slippery spaceship. When he turned back, the wolves were lining up across the bank, their long faces appearing out of the gloom in great numbers.

"Hurry!" Jaric screamed. "Look behind you!"

Then they were struggling against the sides of the smooth ship, and the wolves were splashing off into the reeds. They were all feeling a suffocating panic in the heavy earth-g, and after their run it seemed as if gravity was growing heavier within them.

"Here!" Drewyn said to Saraj, and he folded his hands to make a step for her.

"Yes! Yes!" she cried, and jumped from his hands up onto the ship. Then she lay flat and extended her arm down. By jumping hard each of them reached her grip, which was like a hook of crystal steel, and she quickly yanked them up beside her.

They ran along the side of the spaceship and dropped into the doorway. Drewyn, last, slammed the hatch shut.

In a moment the wolves were swimming all around the spaceports of the ship, growling with slitted eyes and ragged fur, their lips curled back, teeth exposed. "Look at them!" Drewyn said. "They're all over the marsh!"

"There was no end to them," Tamara said, shivering. "You know, I've read all about wolves—they aren't supposed to act like this."

"Unless they're starving," Drewyn said.

They looked out at the nervous, furious animals swimming around them. The wolves snapped at each other in their desire to get down through the windows.

"Well," Jaric said, "we'll have to plan very carefully before we try leaving here."

"You're not kidding," Tamara said.

"Oh, oh," Drewyn said softly.

"What?" Jaric asked.

"A ship," he said, "a small Hovercraft. It just passed over."

"Could it be Mother?" Tamara asked without thinking.

"No," Saraj replied, "your mother doesn't have a ship."

15

"I AM ALL THESE THINGS"

"Are you all right?" Drewyn asked, staring at Saraj.

"The question," Jaric said angrily, "is how does she know what your mother has or doesn't have?" He stepped close to her and looked at her small, pretty face, her clear blue eyes. "*Well?!*" he shouted.

"Tava Langstrom left Moon Island VII on fifteenth April, 2135, in a stolen Starlight Series earthrocket. Hovercraft were not standard equipment aboard those craft, and she didn't have time to acquire one."

They were all silent, breathless, listening and watching Saraj speak as if from within a trance, or even as if someone else were speaking for her—through her—from far away. Jaric was poised with his weight on one foot; even he seemed subdued, unwilling to break her mood. Saraj continued, her eyes alert and yet distant.

"Tava Langstrom picked that particular rocket because it had been outfitted as an exploratory genetics unit, a research vessel, and it contained what she called her 'dream laboratory.'"

Jaric spoke softly, holding back his anger. "When did she say those words?"

Saraj turned slowly to him. "To Ryland Langstrom, the human she . . . loved."

"And how did *you* learn this?"

"It was recorded in their bedchamber, and now it's part of a filetape in Central's library."

"You mean the classified library, the Level Four Overone Eyes-Only Library, don't you?"

"Yes," she said, opening herself to their silence.

"Then why," Jaric said softly, clearing his own dry throat, spreading and tightening his fingers, "why did they let *you* listen to it?"

"You must know that by now," Saraj said. "I'm not a . . . human. I was created by the Overones and programmed to watch all of you. I'm what you call a . . . spy. They wanted me to know all about you, Tamara, so they played me all the tapes on your parents."

"No," Tamara whispered, coming to her. She touched Saraj's cheek, as if to feel for her human essence.

"You saw, when you healed me. My body is not simply flesh and bone and blood like yours, but electronic, too."

"But you're my best friend."

"Yes," Saraj said, "that part is true."

"You may not be *made* just like me, but you have a soul, Saraj."

"Whatever that is," Jaric said sarcastically.

"Tamara's right," Drewyn said. "And we don't have to know what a soul is, to know Saraj has one."

"I never told them anything," Saraj said, her eyes narrowing in anger. Tamara put her arms around Saraj and hugged her, and there were tears against her own cheek.

"What do you *feel?*" Tamara asked.

"That I love you."

"Oh, great," Jaric said, "a robot loves us."

"Listen," Drewyn said slowly and intensely, "remember what Father said about the animal wars on

Old Earth? That when different species were crossed with human genetics they could think and feel as we do? And when they first gained speech and demanded rights—do you remember how they were treated?"

"Of course," Jaric said. "Nobody trusted them. And they were right, too, weren't they? Because the new creatures banded together and rose up against their creators."

"You say 'rose up,'" Tamara answered, "but they were non-violent with their movements, remember? Those times are called the 'animal wars' in Luna's history books, but that's so wrong!"

"Whatever they did," Drewyn continued, "maybe it was because of the way they were treated, and maybe we're treating Saraj the same way, right now."

"You're amazing," Jaric said. "You're willing to risk our lives, and maybe that of your own mother, just for some, some—" He looked at Saraj and shook his head.

"Some what?" she said. "Freak? Robot? Alien? Spy? Experiment? Is that what you think? You'd be right, Jaric, because I am all these things."

Saraj rose and walked to the spaceport and looked up at the sky.

"I was created by the most brilliant of the Overone designers. I was given my existence, and the ability to love, or to feel what I think is love . . . for Tamara . . . and for you. And the only condition I must fulfill is to spy on you and betray you."

She crossed her arms and turned to them, trembling. "Kill me now, if you want to be safe. Go on."

Jaric went for his laser.

"No, you don't!" Drewyn cried, jumping in front of Saraj. Tamara walked straight to Jaric, pushed the laser aside with one hand and slapped him hard with the other.

"She's my *friend*, Jaric!" Tamara said. "Drewyn's right about the Old Earth creatures; Father said it, didn't he? Didn't he and Mother respect them? And weren't they passive resisters to the war that exterminated them?"

"That's what they *said* they were," Jaric hissed. "Some called them cowards." He put the laser away and kicked the spaceship's wall as hard as he could three times. Then, in a moment, when he turned to face them, he was more composed.

"All right, Tamara, we'll have it your way for now. Saraj, you're on probation. If I see you do the slightest thing against us, I'll short circuit you so fast you won't even smell the wires burning, have you got that?"

"Jaric!" Tamara said. "How can you talk so?" She put her arm around Saraj.

"Don't blame him," Saraj said sadly. "I won't betray you, and eventually he'll know that. But there are questions about me . . . even in your mind and in Drewyn's . . . you don't know what I am, and I guess I don't, either."

"That's why this is a new age," Drewyn said, echoing their father. They all held still a moment, remembering him saying this, calling them to the excitement he and their mother had felt for the crosses, the hybrids, all the wealth of new consciousness created by genetic engineers.

"That's right," Tamara said softly. "I'm sure he and Mother would feel exactly the same about Saraj. And as far as I'm concerned, she's still my sister."

Saraj looked at her, and Tamara saw the depth in her eyes and, it seemed, a clarity and intelligence she hadn't perceived before.

"We'd best turn to the question of that Hovercraft," Jaric said.

"I can tell you whose it is," Saraj answered, and Jaric slapped his sides in frustration that she remained so at the center of things. "It belongs to Gorid Malcolm Hawxhurst, who escaped from the moon ten years ago. He also took a Starlight Series rocket, equipped for genetics work, and he had a Hovercraft on board."

"I've heard of him," Drewyn said.

"Yes," Tamara added, "so have I. Wasn't he in charge of the Island V breeding program?"

"That's right," Saraj said, "the hunting project. He created the dune bears your father cared so much for, and countless other species that have now been slaughtered to the last."

"But why would he want to escape?" Jaric asked impatiently. "He had an important job. And didn't he love to make up new species and then hunt them?"

"Yes," Saraj said. "But he wanted to work with all the wild stock left on Old Earth; the Overones got very tired of his enthusiasm—animals mating, stalking and killing animals; they realized he had a purpose they couldn't understand. So they decided the Gorid was a bad example to the young. As far as they were concerned, his program was only a means of recreation for the miners, the cavers, all the human drudges. When robotics began to replace the human workers in those jobs, the Overones decided the Gorid's diversions weren't needed."

"So he escaped to earth, to keep doing the same thing?"

"That's what the Eyes-Only files say."

"That's so similar to Mother's work!" Tamara said.

"Except that she wanted to *preserve* earth's old

species . . . not make up new ones to hunt and kill,"
Drewyn replied.

"Yes . . . but they both had genetics labs on their
ships . . . they both came to work with the animals that
were left . . . I wonder if they've met each other."

"The important point right now," Jaric said, "is that if
it's Gorid Hawxhurst who passed over in the Hovercraft,
what are his intentions toward us?"

"He was a dangerous man," Saraj said. "My guess is
that he'd like to use you for breeding stock; me . . . I
can't imagine . . . don't want to imagine."

"Well," Jaric said, "surely he would have called by now
if he wanted to be friendly. We'd better get ready and get
out of here."

16

AN IMPOSSIBLE PROPOSITION

Gorid Malcolm Hawxhurst flew a wide slow pattern in his Hovercraft, circling the earthrocket two miles out and a mile high. He saw the four young people climbing from their ship into the morning light, and he smiled to see them setting out toward Bestiary Mountain. *How do they know so much*? he wondered. *Never mind . . . let's see how far they get in the marshes; let the wild wolves bay them, humble them on their new planet. Before sundown I'll pluck them without a net.*

Laughing harshly, he turned his little cruiser northward and flew at top speed toward Bestiary Mountain.

A half hour later he caught sight of it, slowed and entered a hailing signal on his transmitter. He floated down and landed in a small, grassy field, and by now there was an answering aural code.

"This is Gorid Hawxhurst, requesting a conference with Doctor Langstrom. Please don't tell me she's too busy, or everyone at Bestiary Mountain will deeply regret it."

"What do you want, Gorid?"

"Ah! The mistress of the mountain herself! May I also have the pleasure of visual contact?"

The screen in his display panel began to warm up, and he flipped the switch to transmit his own image to the castle. In a moment he saw the thin, and to him still beautiful, face of Tava Langstrom.

"What a privilege, my dear! It's been so long."

"Not long enough, Gorid. What is it you want?"

"Chilly, chilly, so chilly. I've come to offer you something beyond your wildest imagination, something for which, I suggest, you'll trade every secret of your lab. Intrigued?"

"Go on."

"You do remember your children, don't you?"

There was silence that felt like static.

"The girl, Tamara, and your little boy Drewyn. You haven't seen them since they were one year old, have you, Doctor?"

"Reach your point."

"They're sixteen now, fine children, if I'm a judge. They've followed in their mother's footsteps and flown to Old Earth in a stolen ship. Imagine! Of course they're my guests now. They were foolish enough to land in my territory."

"Have you proof of this?" Tava asked, her voice rising, strained.

"Proof? *Proof?!* If I have to provide proof, you won't like it."

"Did they come alone?"

"No, my dear, for your information they did not. But their companions will remain with me. I'm only offering your children for sale."

"What did you have in mind?" she asked, her eyes tight.

"Spoken like a reasonable soul! Let's see now, I'll be reasonable, too . . . I won't ask for everything . . . let's say you turn the mountain over to me. Give me your labs, all your animals — and that's including Kana — and in return I'll let you and your children live in my West Valley. You can take anything you like with you, as long as the three of you can carry it on your backs!" He broke into wild laughter.

"Ridiculous," was her bitten-off reply.

"Have it your way, then, *Mother*."

"Wait, Gorid, now listen to me —"

"Your next opportunity will come some hours from now. By then I'll have learned a great deal from my young guests. I'll have taken genetic samples from them for my cryogenic vaults. I may even have run them with my new hounds — equipped with humaniod frontal lobes, *most interesting* — so think it over, dear, do think it over."

"Gorid!" she screamed. But he had already broken off his own image and voice signal and was simply watching her come apart in silence.

He wondered how long it would take her to regain enough dignity to kill her visual transmission.

When his screen went blank, he rotated his Hovercraft and took off again. He'd predicted her response exactly. What a wonderful dilemma for her! Lifelong ideals, scientific commitment, her drastic choice to leave her infants and husband in order to save the earth's fauna . . . suddenly thrown in her face, pitted against her maternal memories! *Not just memories now*, the Gorid thought, grinning. *Your chance to be a mother again, lovely one. And if you turn it down, if you turn it down . . .*

The Gorid slid his teeth together, smiling, as he flew south.

Tava Langstrom took the stone stairs that spiraled upward in her castle, moving fast, sucking quick breaths, rushing as if her solutions lay waiting at the top. When she finally burst through the locked doors and stood trembling on the turret, her dark eyes wild for relief, there was nothing for her to see but the quiet, thick fog of the day. It was chilly and damp above the mountain, and the moving fog-clouds boiled up around her as if to erase the world, or perhaps to mock her violent need. She held out her arms to pray and demand and receive an answer all at once, but she received the Gorid's logic again, his voice inside her head. Maddening! Her vision of the domain was blocked, her vision of her own life was blocked. Would the Gorid make up such an outrageous lie? Without reasoning through it, she knew he hadn't.

If he were lying, surely he would have offered evidence — a photograph or a video, something clever beyond cleverness; a voice tape . . . maybe a hair sample she could analyze for genetic markers . . . even a piece of the alleged earthship. But nothing! *He* is *telling the truth,* she thought. *He's riding the confidence of real hostages, my children.*

She closed her eyes and rubbed her arms. Then she felt her cheeks with her crossed hands, the soft wrinkles of her skin and, beneath, her high cheekbones. If only she could will herself beyond this flesh, make this stone castle-world and this mountain vanish in a flash. In all these lonesome years her battle with the Gorid had never failed to be a challenge, almost a wicked game that kept her alive. Having an enemy like him, with imagination and power, yet with a certain childish naiveté that allowed her to outguess him in the end, had been some sort of substitute for not having a lover, a family, a real life.

She'd never understood, until she took on this romantic and doomed task of saving the old animals and committed herself to solitary struggle on this war-abandoned planet, how much an enemy can mean.

But all that had ended today. Now Gorid Hawxhurst had captured Tamara and Drewyn, and whatever she did would be hopeless. The Gorid had turned it around, from a battle over possession of the new animal lives into a zero-sum game, where winning meant there must be a loser. No matter which way she tried to move, she would destroy herself.

Tamara and Drewyn. In the early days of her separation from them, she'd thought about them all the time, regretting bitterly her decision to leave. If only she could have known how it would hurt. But it was too late. The earthrocket was wrecked beyond repair, and even if she'd had the technology for a return trip to the moon, she would have been executed on sight, lasered out of the artificial skies. Still, all that didn't make the pain less cutting; it was like a constant state of weather, only inside her, a dense and shifting cloud. It had broken down her sense of herself as a mother. But she knew how much she'd accomplished with the animals, and so — feeling now her skin and bones and long hair — the woman had survived. She had escaped turning into a neurotic, driven thing, by the sheer challenge of Malcolm Hawxhurst, and, later, by the company of Kana, and of the Round Beast. She had not become a madwoman, a scientist enslaved to a dream, but had remained warm and capable, once in a great while, of laughing. At least she thought she had won out. She still dreamed of her husband and believed that, if by miracle he were restored to her, she would easily and joyfully be his wife again.

A pair of crows flew past her silently in the fog.

Even you, she thought to them, *need me here. And if I am destroyed today, then so, one day soon, you will be also.*

Her children! How could this *be?!* How could they, of all humans and creatures on two worlds, reappear to her now? *Is it to mock the pain I've felt for them so long?* With each passing year that pain had dulled just a little. At first she'd wondered why, and for a while—when the kids were twelve, for some reason—the growing relief she seemed to feel was overwhelmed by a new rush of guilt. After all, what kind of mother abandons her children for the salvation of other species, then gradually outgrows her suffering for them?

But just in the past year—as they'd turned sixteen—a whole new feeling about them had appeared. She worried less, trusting that Ryland had done well, and trusting them, too. Even though she didn't even know them, she had a strange, serene confidence in their spirits. And one day, when she was down in the chamber of the Round Beast communing, the right words had suddenly come to her. Her year-by-year relief corresponded to the normal course of a parent's life. If she were with them now, worrying over them as if they were infants—that would be crazy. For better or worse, they were growing up; and as they did, her own choices about them, her actions that were past, completed, finished, cast in a kind of sculpture—yes, time-sculpture, that was it—those actions, mercifully, took on a less urgent presence and weight.

And now this! If they have come, why *have they come? Can it be to*—and then she knew in the instant that they had come to find her, that they loved her.

Tava's stomach was churning and it was hard to concentrate. The world she had built all alone, in the isolation of fifteen years, was to be yanked away from her in one hour. If she failed to bargain for her children and they were lost to the Gorid's captivity, her life was over. Yet, if she gave Gorid Hawxhurst her laboratories, her creatures, the power of her work and Kana—her living masterpiece—and, most unthinkable of all, the key to the chamber of the Round Beast, then she would betray all she had lived for. Besides, everything she knew about the Gorid said that he'd never leave them in peace—not even a pitiful, primitive peace in the caves of the West Valley. He'd use them for sport, as objects of stalking, or as a game for his hybrid thinking hounds.

So there was no way to win. She couldn't bargain, and she'd never be able to lure the Gorid into a deathtrap she'd set for him.

In that light, it was time to think of dying, both for herself and for her children. *If he really has them prisoner,* she realized, *he'll never let them survive my attack.*

And that thought led her to the next revelation, opening like a door in the boiling white fog: perhaps she could kill the Gorid, too. At least, if she succeeded, the earth would be left for the animals, the remnants of old kinds, as well as her own recreants—and even the Gorid's new monsters. Without his sporting slaughters, Tava thought, the animals would have Old Earth again, and who knows where evolution might go next time.

Yes, she whispered aloud with her solitary and practiced resolve. *It is time to think differently, all right*— not like a woman clinging to her skin and her hopes; not like a scientist or a restorer of species and certainly not like a coward before the Gorid's might.

It is time to think like a warrior. To use these fifteen

years of struggle, and what they've built inside me. To think of death for myself and my family. To think of death with honor and — one last achievement, to cast in the time-sculpture — of death for my enemy as well.

17

TO THE MOUNTAIN

Jaric led the others up out of the spacecraft. It was noon, warm and mild, and they were guessing the wolves would be asleep. So they hurried out, closed the hatch and walked down the long, slippery surface of the ship. They jumped off into the water, this time soberly and watchfully, and made their way toward the thick pines.

When they reached the low cliff they found a narrow path and followed it. Wolf tracks were everywhere, so they set out as fast as they could northward, alert to attack from all directions. Jaric carried the laser; the others armed themselves with the best sticks they could find.

They traveled steadily for an hour, skirting the swamp to the northwest, then moving easily through heavy timber that had shaded out most of the brush. It occurred to Saraj that these were bigger trees than any she'd seen in the library books about Old Earth, and it must be because, since the wars and the exodus, there'd been nobody to cut them down. She walked third in line, behind Tamara, with Drewyn behind her. It would seem strange to anyone else, but this arrangement gave her an eerie excitement and security. She'd never had a childhood like the others, since she'd been created in the

Overones' laboratory at her present age. Her designer had spoken of Saraj having her own brain engrams, and that must mean some kind of childhood memories, of whatever life the designer had experienced, but there didn't seem to be any at all. Saraj's whole world began with the training sessions on Moon Island II, the indoctrinations that were part lectures, part programming-tranfusions and part practicum exams. In these she had to interact with humans — or what she believed were humans — to see how well she could pass for one of them. The hardest thing was emotions, since the humans had built theirs up from childhood; Saraj was quick at learning to read their behavior and to pretend her own responses were from the heart. But the mysterious thing was that they *were*. This was her great secret from her creators, one she didn't understand. She could act angry or loving because she really felt both, really wanted to show those human states. And it was hard to believe her designer didn't know that. Still, she didn't seem to. And Saraj sensed it would be unwise to ever tell. So she had a real nervous system in a flesh-and-blood body, in spite of the chips and wires that also made her. And her feelings grew all the time, attaching more and more deeply to Saraj and Drewyn, whose friendship encompassed her only memories that weren't built on games in Overone lab school, the only memories she could trust. Walking between them in the shady, powerful oakwoods of Old Earth, then, gave her a sense of simple childhood placing, of fitting in and of being filled with feelings about who she was, or who she *should* have been, had she been completely a person.

The first wolf came at her from her right side, and she just had time to swing her stick high and crack it across its wet nose in mid-leap. The animal fell beside her, sprawling and kicking and jerking, blood streaming out of its nose under pressure. The other wolves slowed up at the sight of their helpless leader, giving Jaric a chance to draw his laser pistol and take steady aim. He blasted the first of them with a stream of green fire, then another and another, and the remainder of the scroungy pack ran yelping into the trees.

Tamara led them in an examination of the dead wolves. They were starving, their bones all but sticking through their fur.

"But why?" Drewyn asked. "This woods seems so rich; you'd think there'd be plenty of rabbits and things for them to eat."

"Yeah," Jaric said. "Maybe there're too many wolves. Or maybe something else eats the rabbits."

"If that's it," Tamara added, "perhaps we should take their meat — we don't want to end up looking like them."

"That's true," Jaric said.

"They look sick," Drewyn said. "Surely we can find something better."

Tamara turned to Saraj. "Any ideas?"

"Let's go on," Saraj said. "Did you see how hard I hit that wolf?"

"Yes."

"I did, too, as a matter of fact," Drewyn said.

"I have a lot more strength than I've ever shown you," Saraj said. "And I can run faster than you would imagine. If we have to hunt, I can help quite a lot."

"Oh, great," Jaric said. "Now we're more or less at the mercy of the robot."

"Stop talking like that!" Tamara cried. "I won't have it anymore! Do you hear me?"

"Maybe I should just turn my laser over to her, too, Tamara. Would that make you happy? Take away the only defense we seem to have."

"I suggest we get moving," Drewyn said. "The wolves may change their minds."

"Good idea," Tamara said. "Jaric?"

"Yeah. Sure." He led again, walking so fast that the others had to jog to keep up.

They kept going silently for another hour, then stopped to rest on the side of a rolling hill. The country was growing steeper, with low blue mountains rising in the northward distance. They could see, now, they'd been traveling up the forested side of a great valley, which ran south to north. There were reddish sage fields stretching below them.

"Might as well keep this course," Drewyn said. "Everyone agree?"

"Yes," Tamara said.

"Check with the machine," Jaric sneered.

They both glanced away from him, not wanting to join the argument. All they could think about was how much he had changed. And even though they didn't want to hold it against him, they were growing sick of it.

The next time they stopped to rest, Drewyn stretched out in the grass and held up the empty plastic bottle. "So far," he said, "I haven't seen a bit of water. And we'd better find some soon."

"Yeah," Tamara said.

"How about you?" Jaric asked Saraj. "You ever need a drop of water? Or would that short out your brains?"

"I need a little," she said sadly.

Tamara stood up and raised her stick. She started toward him as Drewyn grabbed her. "Tamara! What's the matter with you? You don't want to start acting like him."

She glanced at the two of them for a moment, then sank down on the grass.

"We'd better stop trudging so fast," Drewyn said, "and hunt food and water, and a place to camp."

"Yes," Saraj added. "We don't know how far we have to go—it may take days or even weeks."

"Look!" Tamara whispered, pointing across the field below.

There was a patch of grass just before the sage field ended in trees, and everyone saw a big rabbit hopping across it.

"I'll catch it," Saraj said. "Wait here."

"Yes, *ma'am*," Jaric said bitterly as she jogged off down the hill.

"Jaric," Tamara said very gently after a moment.

"Yeah?"

"Sometimes we can't see things about ourselves . . . things our friends can see, you know?"

"Un-huh."

"Please don't get mad at me when I just try to talk with you about this."

"Saraj?"

Tamara nodded.

"We have no way of knowing what she'll do. She could change at any second and revert to some weird computer loyalty. Really, Tamara, I can't believe the way you and Drewyn keep acting."

"Father always said to give every life form a chance," Drewyn said in a rising tone.

"Well, he never said anything about risking *my* life doing it, did he?"

"No," Tamara said. "No . . . you're right about that."

"She gives me the creeps," Jaric added.

Drewyn slammed his fist into the soft dirt and turned away.

"There she is," Tamara said.

Saraj was standing at the edge of the trees waving at them. Not only was she holding up the rabbit, but it was already skinned and cleaned for cooking.

"There's a little stream in the woods," she said as they reached her. "I've gathered wood for a fire."

"Handy," Jaric said. "Can you light a fire, too?"

"No."

"Well, well." He reached in his pocket and pulled out a small plastic container; he unscrewed its top and produced a wooden match. "Humans are sometimes clever in their own little ways," he said.

When they had eaten the roasted rabbit and drunk from the clear stream and rested, late evening pinks were stretched softly across the sky.

"We'd better find a place to camp," Drewyn said.

"Not down in this streambed," Jaric replied. "All the animals in these woods must roam along here at night, if water is as scarce as it seems."

"Let's head up the slope then."

They extinguished their fire and started up the sage-grass hillside, when the Hovercraft appeared as a dot on the horizon. It flew straight toward them, too fast for them to escape, and when it was within a hundred yards it came to a quick stop and then gradually circled. They stood, watching, their only possible defense being the laser pistol tucked out of sight under Jaric's shirt.

"Do you think it's that Gorid?" Tamara asked.

"Shhhh!" Jaric said, and she remembered that a Hovercraft had the capacity to hear them at this distance.

Finally it flew to a spot directly above them and stopped.

Then a small envelope drifted down, spinning, and landed beside them. Inside there was a printed note that read: MY NEW HOUNDS HAVE THE FRONTAL LOBES OF HUMANITY. THEY HAVE NEVER RUN HUMANS BEFORE, AND I WOULD NOT LIKE THEM TO START SO LATE IN THE DAY. SO YOU HAVE ONE MORE NIGHT ON MY PLANET. GOOD LUCK. THE CHASE BEGINS AT DAWN.

When they looked up again, the Hovercraft was flying fast, and it disappeared over the northeast ridge.

18 _____

Tava Langstrom knocked on the heavy oak door of Kana's chamber. As she waited, she felt the coldness rising in her throat again. It made no sense, but for months now she'd miss Kana when she was away from him, yet be overtaken with anger the moment she saw him. She had never been this way to anyone, and she knew how the harshness of her words must hurt Kana; it was almost as if some warning about him were sounded deep in her unconscious.

He opened the door looking surprised—normally she simply summoned him—and he admitted her graciously. His living room was spotlessly neat, painted in cool greens and blues, and there were branches of deep-green magnolia leaves in tall clay pots.

"Kana, we have some hard decisions to make," she said, and she walked around his room restlessly, taking it all in but without the pleasure Kana had hoped to see.

She told him about the Gorid's offer.

"So you see," she concluded, "our old enemy has managed to destroy me at last. If I exchange the children for everything here"—she opened her arms to indicate the castle-world—"then at best we'll be reduced to cave mammals in the West Valley. But in fact, you know as well as I, we'd be nothing but hound-prey for the Gorid's experimental packs. And you also know we'd never survive a rescue attempt."

Kana was still, his eyes pools of green glass.

"For myself," Tava said, "I'm preparing to attack and die. I can't ask that of you, but there's one choice you must make. You can stay here and defend the castle—I'll destroy the labs, but everything else is yours—or we can blow the whole thing to bits and you can set out on your own. You might travel beyond the Gorid's sphere, Kana, and find yourself some kind of a life."

Alert and absorbing, Kana felt himself sliding into the cat's way, using his human intelligence coldly and automatically, with a great simplicity. The emotions of this time would fly later; for now there must be processing, comparing, seeking an opening in the Gorid's new battle-spread.

"Don't plan without me," Kana said quietly, letting a slight masculine purr roll over his voice.

"Think what you're saying," Tava said.

Kana flushed with embarrassment.

"I have spoken," he said, turning his cat's eyes away from the intensity of her own.

"Well," she said, rising, "I just want you to be sure. Don't throw your life away too quickly. I'm going to the Round Beast now, so you'll have a little while to think it over."

With that she hurried out.

When the door clicked shut, Kana leapt from his sofa and shot into his bedroom. Here he kept the tall cedar scratching post that he needed for times like this. He attacked it with his unsheathed claws, pulling down deeply into the heartwood, raking and tearing, letting his mind go blank and his instinct run loose. He had offered her his life, and all she could say was think it over while I go to the Round Beast! Shavings curled from the wood and fell around him.

Finally, tired, he pulled back from the torn, good-smelling post and was overwhelmed with human shame at his explosion. It was the two-being bitterness he knew so well, and even though he understood it better now than he used to, that didn't make it change. But this! This was the final insult from Tava, his creator, his goddess. Kana walked to the window and glared into the moving fog. Why had she created him? He asked himself again and again. She'd once said she was repelled by the Gorid's practice of playing with genetics, making up new species just to hunt them or to use them as if they were dog packs. Her own work was supposed to be the restoration and recovery of earth's old ones, the terminated kinds, or those with only a few living members. Then why had she created him at all?

Alone, no female or even male companion in existence, he seemed to live only to serve her. And in his loneliness, Kana had come to crave her company; he needed it more than water and food, and he couldn't understand her coldness to him. He realized now that even in his final service, his willingness to die with her, even now she would not open herself to him. She kept her words to the barest few, and she still preferred the Round Beast to him. That Round Beast! It never emerged from its chamber, it had never wanted to see Kana and it took more and more of Tava's time. What was it, anyway? This was the deepest sting of all, that she had never confided the secret of the Round Beast to Kana, her protector, her most trusted friend.

Kana's stomach turned over and over. For the first time, he wondered whether Tava was worth dying for.

Tamara, Saraj, Jaric and Drewyn were on top of the ridge under the half moon. A cold breeze blew over them, died, then picked up again.

"I still think we should go back to the ship," Drewyn said. "We could make it by dawn, and those dogs would never get us in there."

"We'd have to pass by starving wolves in the dark," Tamara said. And the Gorid is probably waiting back that way with a trap."

"Besides," Jaric said, "we've been all through that, and we've voted no. It's better if we stick to our plan—to stay beneath the trees and keep moving north toward your mother. If the dogs find us I can still use this." He held up the laser, with its fading power packs.

"I can kill dogs very well," Saraj said. "You'll see."

"Saraj," Tamara said, "you're a lot different to me now—different than when we roomed together in the dormpound. That seems like a lifetime ago."

"It was," Saraj said quietly.

"Were you as fast and as strong then?"

"Not like I am now—but I pretended to be much weaker than I really was."

"What made you change?"

"When the designer scanned me and replaced some chips, she increased my physical powers for a better act-to-risk ratio."

"What's that?"

"You see, I could be programmed for a level of strength that would hurt me. But before, I was set up to appear as a fragile young girl. Now it's about right."

"Why were you 'set up' that way?" Drewyn asked.

"To fool Tamara, and all of you. That's why my grades weren't so great, too, remember?" She laughed for the first time since their landing.

"Beta-minus!" Tamara said. "Poor little Saraj!" They laughed together.

"Did you even need to be in school?" Tamara asked.

"No."

"What a scheme!" Tamara said. "They thought I was that important?"

"Look what you did," Saraj said.

"Yeah," Drewyn laughed, "you stole a spaceship and flew it here successfully. They were on the right track about you."

"And you, too."

"It was because of your parents," Saraj said. "You see, they accomplished things that amazed the Overones. The Overones are afraid it's genetic—the ability to surprise them."

"Good," Drewyn said. "Let them go on thinking that. Someday, I'm going to surprise them again."

"Yeah?" Jaric said.

"Yeah. I'm going back for Father."

They were all silent then. It sounded so foolish, so helpless against the night wind and the clear, starry sky. Their ship would never fly again. The trip to Old Earth had been the most unlikely feat of their lives. And yet, Drewyn's having had the confidence to express their wish aloud . . . it gave them all courage, and a sense that these humanoid-hounds weren't such an impossible problem and certainly wouldn't be the end of them.

"We'd better get some sleep," Jaric finally said.

"Everybody remember the plan?" Saraj asked quietly.

"I sure do," Tamara said.

"Me, too," Drewyn said. "When the hounds come, up in the trees for us. Saraj fights with her stick on the ground as long as she can. Jaric saves his laser for the Gorid."

"That's it," Saraj said.

Jaric walked over into the trees without a word.

Tamara said good night and headed down the ridge to a pine thicket she had picked out.

Drewyn and Saraj stood together for a moment.

"Well," Drewyn said awkwardly, "we'd better sleep a little, too."

"Drewyn?"

"Yes."

"Would you stay with me for a minute?"

"Sure, Saraj."

They sat down side by side, and Drewyn put his arm around her. His mind raced with the warmth of her, and with a million questions. It excited him to hold her so close, and to not quite know what she was.

"The last time we were together," Saraj said, "you kissed me."

She looked straight ahead.

Gently, Drewyn touched her far cheek with his finger and turned her face to his. In a moment she put her head on his shoulder.

Drewyn felt a warm tear on his neck.

"What is it?"

"The same thing it's been with you, ever since you found out . . . wondering if you can still care for me."

"Of course I do."

"Quick words, Drewyn, but I know it must be strange for you."

"You are what you do, not where you came from."

"I hope so, I really hope so. Because . . . you know, up until now, I've had this kind of double existence. I was a spy for the Overones, and I was Tamara's — and your — friend."

"Yes."

"Well, both were true lives for me. And they were coexistent, simultaneous, even compatible . . . until they came into direct conflict. All the earlier robotic series were designed strictly on Aristotelian-Russellian logic, and a conflict would be easily, and clumsily, decided."

"In favor of the Overones."

"That's right. But I'm different. I have a deeper logic, based in the human engrams of my designer, rather than in the dyadic impulses of chips."

Drewyn hugged her and listened closely.

"My designer called it dialectical logic . . . but that's just a name, because she didn't really know how it would work in the critical case — when her own value-program became just one of the terms in the dialectic. Now that's happened, and I've resolved it — dissolved it — in a new synthesis of my own creation."

"Which is joining us?"

Saraj felt a stab of pain. "Not just joining you. And not pretending to be one of you. I'm seeking for the words, Drewyn."

"You're one of us," Drewyn said. "Isn't that really it?"

"Yes! I'm one-of-you, bonded-to-you. But I'm not pretending anymore, and that's so different! At least, it feels different to me."

"Yes, that makes sense, sure."

"But I have a terrible danger inside."

"A what?"

"The Overone spy life is finished, and yet it was my primary engram-pattern, the basis of my programming . . . it was my mother and father, as you might say. Now that burden is transferred to your small group. And so—even though I'm so strong and fast physically—my selfness, if that's the right word—?"

"Self. Selfhood. Selfness is okay."

"My selfness depends on you. I could be shattered if you hated me, just as I could shatter your body with one blow."

Drewyn was quiet.

"I see . . ." he said finally. "What about Jaric? Did he upset you when he was so harsh?"

"Oh, yes. But he wasn't you or Tamara. I had to re-program myself quickly, to separate him from the selfness of myself."

"From the . . . you can do that?"

"With him I could, but not with you."

"I see." He squeezed her hand, and they were silent for a moment. "Well," he said, "you don't have to worry about us."

"I hope not," she said, "because I couldn't stand it. I couldn't live. Do you understand?"

"Uh, I think so."

"Good," she said, snuggling tighter against him. "I feel so much better now."

Drewyn felt a kind of panic he had never known before.

19

FIGHTING LIVES

In the first gray light of dawn, a single hound came trotting up the spine of the ridge. He wasn't howling or barking, just silently and quickly following their cold trail from the night before. When he winded fresh scent of their bodies on the morning breeze, he felt the complex signal all the way through him as a shock, a mistake, a stubborn, bright datum mixing up his gut and brain. Without thinking, he had already skidded to a stop, and he cocked his huge head, catching the smells of different animals, close together, sleep-warm, bedded-smelling, easy to surprise — stupid? — and too close to last night's beginning-place.

The rabbits and deer and foxes this enormous dog had run before had all given him and his pack hard chase, full of the treachery of stream-tricks, wild, circling patterns, earth-tunneling or tree-climbing. But this new prey didn't run, and it slept lazily while he silently bore down!

He turned and ran fast the half mile to his pack. The eleven of them were coming slowly to meet him, waiting to hit stride for his signal-wail that the new-prey had been jumped. But he told them with whines and eager scratches in the dirt what a strange victim-group this was, either foolish and vulnerable and ready to die, or laying some trap beyond his experience. The other dogs listened and let themselves flow into the communal, moiling, deep-gut pack decision, resisting the hottest-headed and the afraid-ones alike, deciding finally on the fear-force of a pack-wail and racing off joyfully in their brotherhood-sisterhood-strength. Roaring and howling and frothing and yelping helplessly with excitement, they fused together into one kill-hot raging mind, loving each other as parts of a single living heart, pouring faster and faster over the ridge, each possessed by the blindness of a personal need, to tear and eat a rightful portion of the new-prey.

In this moment the invented hounds were truly canine beasts, and if their partly humanoid brains had slowed them a moment before in forms of deliberation, those same advanced processes now gave way to the ancient hunting needs of the much older hound brains, adding no longer reason, but a reckless humanoid frenzy to the animal rush.

Tamara, lying across the broad limbs of the oak tree she had sleepily climbed at the first warning of the pack's din, heard the noise boil and grow until it froze her inside, left her weak and motionless, a waiting innocent paralyzed before the oncoming wall of sound. Then she saw them. Tall and quick, short haired and black with tan mottles, tumorous lumps rising above their eyes—bone shields of the new brain tissue—they covered the earth in great leaps. They seemed to move with such ease, pulling themselves by hard knots of exposed muscles like those of Dobermans she had seen in books. But these were more like an ancient European breed, staghounds or wolfhounds, modified horribly by those grotesque structures of their square, alert, snapping and blathering heads.

Suddenly they were beneath her, criss-crossing and growling and then spotting her, jumping up and up to rake away bark in ragged strips, biting into the oak-meat and shaking their whole lengths as they tore chunks from the tree.

Tamara's mind was chilled, unmoving; their plan seemed hopeless before this living maze of dog-demons. Surely Saraj would abandon the idea of fighting them and climb for her life. But suddenly she ran in amongst the beasts, and they jumped back as if shocked by this small, quick, silent being who mocked their strength. Saraj swung her stick over her head, and the hounds flinched in their circle. Then, seizing the last instant of surprise, Saraj stepped forward and smashed the nearest dog to the ground. The others stared at it jerking and bleeding, and Saraj started for the next of them. But her stick was broken now, and she flung it away as she caved in a hound's face with a karate kick. The pack was screaming in kill-frenzy mixed with a new anxiety of fear, and they tightened their circle around her with their wet teeth exposed, their splotched gums aching and trembling, but their gigantic brains held them to a miserable crawl and blocked the primitive impulse to risk everything. Like programmed automata, they were processing two wildly different signals, to attack and to retreat. The leader broke through the looping circuitry of his own conflicted mind with a great leap in the air, coiling and then sending his tight, heavy frame high in an arc descending onto the thin body of Saraj. She did a cartwheel out from under him and up over the nearest dog, landing cleanly outside their circle of death. Then they massed and charged her as a wall of screaming, barking hound flesh, resolved in closeness to each other, their shoulders feeling electrically bound and bonded so that they really were one entity now, for whatever fate lay next. Saraj was directly beneath Tamara's tree, and she leapt straight up, higher than any human could, catching the limb beside her friend and swinging herself into a comfortable prone position beside her.

Tamara shook as she tightened her grip on the tree.

"They're horrible!" she screamed, still not believing Saraj was alive and as safe as she was in the oak.

The hounds had discovered Drewyn and Jaric in their tree, which was a maple fifty feet up the ridge, and the pack suddenly broke off from the girls and surrounded it. Jaric aimed the laser, even though he had promised to save it, but before he could fire one of the dogs sailed straight up in a sleek, shining explosion of black-and-tan muscle and ripped it from his hand. The hound fell back to earth crunching and gnashing it, landing hard, then jumping up to shake the gun furiously, tossing it and snapping it up in tighter and tighter grips, his mouth bleeding as he tried to smash the metal to bits, and finally he just spit it out, spun around and kicked his hind legs at it in canine disgust and despair.

Then the beasts ran around and around the two trees, frothy and full of the smell of their prey, at first whining in the spirit of wishful hounds, then quickly drawing quiet and still, their humanoid reaches telling them about futility and embarrassment, about regrouping and replanning, about shutting up and waiting as they had been trained with the shock collars to do. They were to tree their quarry and guard it and wait. If they didn't do that they would pay a terrible price in electrical pain. So within a few minutes they became statues, ranged around the trees in perfect circles, sentinels that might have been cast in the limestone of the mountain ridge.

And soon enough, the Gorid came.

He was tall and heavyset, with thick gray hair that fell to his shoulders, and his beard was gray and white. He had strong lines in his ruddy skin and a commanding presence that surrounded his bright blue eyes. Behind him, coming out of the trees, was a huge ram.

"Well, well," he said, "moon children."

He looked with distaste at his two dead hounds, then with displeasure at the living ones who watched him out of the corners of their eyes.

"These new creatures of mine aren't what I thought they were," he said after a moment. "The mix wasn't right. You just never know until you try."

He walked beneath the girls and studied them.

"You," he said, pointing at Saraj. "I saw how well you fought. Are you human? Surely they can't make robots as good as you."

"I'm organic," Saraj said.

"Organic! And electronic?"

"Yes."

"My, my, my! Science does march along. Well, I specialize in hybrids myself, pretty one. You'll see. *You'll see!*" He laughed for the first time, a private exploding laugh, too crazy and intense. "Yes," he said when he was calm and frowning again. "You're the one that interests me. So, you're a fighter, eh? Would you like to fight for your freedom?"

"Leave her alone!" Drewyn yelled from his tree.

"If you want to help her, come on down, young man," the Gorid said. He waved his arm in invitation. The hounds crawled a step closer to Drewyn, watching him, shifting their jaws.

The ram walked silently up beside the Gorid. He was enormous, with deeply intelligent eyes.

"We will all have plenty of time to talk later!" the Gorid yelled to everyone. "For now . . . I want to see what this one can do"—he pointed up at Saraj—"against my ram! Do you accept?"

"What are the alternatives?" Saraj asked coolly.

"Ah, ha! Yes, alternatives. Well, let me see . . . if you should win, all of you may go free. We will be neighbors on this vast and rather empty planet."

"And if I lose?"

"In that unfortunate event, my dear, all of you will remain my prisoners."

"Don't do it!" Drewyn yelled to Saraj. "He's lying! Can't you see that? We've got nothing to gain by your fighting!"

But Saraj dropped lightly to the ground.

"Let's find out," she said with a slight smile.

The Gorid and his dogs moved quickly out of her way, and the ram lowered his head and eased sideways, pawing the dirt and beginning to snort.

Saraj looked confident as she turned to follow his circling, her arms moving in a defensive karate pattern, her eyes fixed on his.

Then he charged full out, and it looked to Tamara as if Saraj was finished, for the ram's bulk and speed added up to a terrible rocket of mass-energy firing point-blank at the small girl. Saraj took the ram's horns in her invisibly fast hands and somersaulted over the beast's back, landing on her feet behind him, spinning to face him again. But he was rocketing on down the side of the ridge into the gooseberry bushes and jagged stones, butting this way and that, trying to find the missing target he had never felt on his battering head.

Saraj smiled at the Gorid and resumed her karate stance as the ram came flying back up the slope. This time he ran in close and circled her rapidly, snorting and stamping, eyes full of rage. He lunged at her and twisted in an upsweep of curving horns, trying to gore and butt her at once. She nimbly backed away from him, clawing the air to taunt him, and when he was angry enough to rush mindlessly ahead, she jumped up and placed both hands on his muscular back and passed over him in a cartwheel.

This time he spun about and charged again, desperate at being so mocked before the Gorid. She ran at him and lifted in a flying kick, delivering it to the ram's face, but his forward momentum knocked her sideways and she fell hard. The ram turned, unfazed, pounced onto her back and butted her shoulders down into the rocky ground over and over again. She tried to roll out from under him but she was pinned by his sharp hooves and great weight. Her breath was going fast and something was damaged in her back. Again and again the mass of ram horns smashed her into the earth, shocking the sense from her. She tried to throw herself over but she couldn't move at all, and the pounding wouldn't stop, wouldn't stop, wouldn't stop, wouldn't stop, wouldn't stop.

20

FIREFIGHT

Tava Langstrom and Kana left Bestiary Mountain flying a two-hundred-year-old helicopter. They had salvaged and rebuilt it long ago, kept it in working order, and sometimes Tava warmed it up on the castle's launchpad and even lifted off for a minute or two. This was just to keep it working, against the emergency she never really expected. And here it was.

They were armed with machine guns and hand grenades, all sorts of ancient-earth war weapons they'd found lying about, and they had a far more modern remote-control device rigged, so that, with the activation of three switches in proper sequence, they could blow the castle and its laboratories to dust. The Round Beast himself had designed the mechanism, and it required his cooperation at the other end. If he decided not to blow it, and to risk falling into the Gorid's net, that was his decision. But Tava was ready to die.

Tava and Kana flew south as fast as the machine would go, homing on coordinates the Round Beast had given her. He had also told her when to go, sensing in his inner tissues that the Gorid's energy—and that of his closest creatures—was turned away from them. "This is the moment your children are fighting him," the Round Beast had said. "It is also the best chance you've had in years to surprise him."

Tava had stood before the Round Beast in her black warrior's garb, bulletproof vest and helmet, like an old twentieth-century S.W.A.T.-team member.

"Do you see me returning?" she asked.

"I feel you not caring," he said.

"Don't read my mind," she snapped. "I can do that for myself."

"Your despair is your strength," he said.

"You're giving me wise aphorisms," she said. "I don't need wise aphorisms."

"Beware of Kana," the Round Beast said.

"Kana! What are you talking about? He's absolutely loyal to me."

"He has been."

"So, what? What do you see?"

"He is frustrated. He needs more of your attention; we have spoken of this before."

"I've told you what happens . . . I have the warmest feelings for him, and then when I see him . . ."

"Yes, I've been working on this. It may not all be your fault."

"What does that mean?"

"I will have answers soon. Go now, and be careful."

"Good-bye," Tava said.

She turned crisply and walked out, closing the tall doors carefully as she went. When they clicked shut, the finality of this parting slapped through her. But it helped, too; if life here was finished and this was her last vision of the Round Beast—her guide and counselor and friend all these years—then it was time to face that. And the emptiness surrounding her, like an invisible gas, draining her meaning-energy away, also gave her the aura and presence of the fey. That was it, she remembered, as she set the prop of the old helicopter in motion. When the knights in the Middle Ages prepared for battle the next day, they were said to be fey—ready for death, and hence beyond the pricks and stings of life. Nothing could touch them once they were prepared.

"Tava?" Kana said softly.

"What?!" she snapped, resenting the intrusion.

"Nothing!" he replied, turning to his window.

I must control this, she thought. But something clouded her feelings, made her want to think of anything else. Still, she knew it was absolutely necessary to say something kind now to poor Kana who had never harmed her in his life, and who was willing to die with her.

"We'll come through this," she said. It wasn't what she meant.

"And return to our lives?" he said.

"Just fly," she said.

She shook her head violently from side to side, trying to clear something away. But no matter how she tried to avoid it, being with Kana upset her, brought out a woman she more than disliked.

Now, flying hard over the low mountains in the range, she thought of another secret of the fey knights. Facing the likelihood of death, each sight of earth became painfully sweet and sharp. The air itself, blue and clean today, seemed washed with magical rain, cleansed and purified and redeemed. She could feel the living spirits of the trees spread over the slopes below, the heartbeats of deer in their shadows.

And she felt Kana's love for her, too. He was her success at the forbidden game of mixing human genes with those from an Old Earth species pool. She and Ryland had agreed not to do that, but to dedicate their lives to the preservation of species. Had he violated that trust as well? After the Gorid had done it, creating the ram to oversee his unholy menagerie, she had decided her danger was too great. And the experiment had proven far more successful than she'd dreamed—Kana was smart and sensitive, possessed of a moral sense as refined as that of any human. He was her ideal helper. Then one day, after the first intense year of his training, she had realized how much they cared for each other. They were coming up the western grade in the sunset, returning to the castle after a long walk in which she had told him about the moon, Ryland, and the violation of her promise not to play with human genes. Kana had taken her hand in his own furry paw-hand, the pads strong and warm and sensitive, and by his silent presence he had solidified and sealed what they both felt.

But it unsettled Tava. She fought it as she had fought the loneliness before Kana existed. But nothing, it seemed, could change the bond that grew between them. Nothing for a long time. Then she began waking in the mornings with headaches and a bitter taste and angry dreams about Kana. Why, all of a sudden? Surely it was nothing he'd done. He had no choice, nowhere to go, no one else to *be* except her devoted one. There would never be another soul he could love, unless she created a female for him. And somehow she had always been afraid to do that.

So their relationship had grown more and more strained as the years passed, and of course she could feel Kana's despair rising. But disloyalty? For the first time, Tava was positive the Round Beast was wrong. *Perhaps* he's *become jealous now, just as Kana is so jealous of him!*

Anything's possible in the emptiness of Bestiary Mountain, Tava thought.

They came into sight of the woods where their coordinates crossed, and Tava said, "Get ready." Kana checked his machine gun.

They wouldn't have a chance if the Gorid discovered them and met them in the air. His Hovercraft was laser armed and much faster than their helicopter. So they came over high and fast, looking for any glint of metal in the morning sunlight, any movement beneath the trees. Kana saw it first, the Hovercraft sitting in a little meadow on the slope below; as they drove for it they saw the circle of figures a hundred yards away, atop the ridge. Lower and lower they dropped from the sky, and Tava saw the Gorid running, his silver hair flying behind him, and then she saw the ram bolting ahead, racing for the ship. Kana opened his window, pulled the antique grenade's pin and flung it toward the Hovercraft. It exploded on the ground nearby, and Tava was already banking into a turn to intercept the Gorid. Kana dropped two more grenades and Tava pulled up sharply as they fell in long arcs. She heard them go off, and when she looked again she saw the Gorid and his ram prone on the grass. Tava hesitated, wanting to make another pass at the Hovercraft and destroy it, but instead she descended and skimmed the trees from which the Gorid had run. In a few moments she was suspended over the spot where her children were treed by the humanoid-hounds, and the dogs were running around and around two oaks, their long canine ears blown back by prop wash and their heads snapping in panic-barking against the pounding roar. But they didn't run away, as ordinary hounds would have done, she thought.

Tava dropped as low as she could, then pointed to the

rope ladder. Kana nodded. With his machine gun strapped over his shoulder, he threw the ladder and in a second was out in the window and descending.

In a few moments he was level with Tamara, and only a few feet from her. With his legs locked in the rope ladder, he swung the machine gun into position and aimed at the nearest hound. The dogs were clustered below him now, wild with his cat's smell, knowing in their superior brains that something terrible was about to transpire. Kana opened fire, spraying and spraying them as they rushed at him and leapt high and fell. The ground was littered with their twisting and still forms, and Kana kept firing and firing, heat waves rising off his barrel, until not one was left standing.

Within minutes everyone had climbed aboard the helicopter, Kana carrying the limp and unconscious form of Saraj over his shoulder, and when he slammed the door shut there was still no sign of the Gorid. Tava lifted from their hover and angled high out over the valley. When she was clear she saw that the Gorid and his ram were gone. "Let's finish off the ship!" Kana cried. He shook the grenade in his hand. Tava nodded. But as she banked toward the Hovercraft it began to move. It was off the grass now, unstable, its wings tipping to and fro, and instead of flying into pursuit of Tava it was floating off south. "It's crippled!" Kana yelled. "Go after it! We'll finish it now!"

But Tava wasn't sure. One shot from its lasers and they would be the ones finished. She turned back north, climbing for home.

As she flew she kept turning and staring, smiling, meeting her children's eyes and then reaching to touch their hands as well.

Tamara leaned close and yelled against the chopper noise, "Is it really you? Tava?"

"Of course! Tamara?"

"Yes! Who else?"

They laughed together. Drewyn squeezed Tava's arm and she met his eyes. "You look like your father!" she shouted. He nodded. "That's what they say!"

She looked in her mirrors but there was no sign of pursuit.

She kept checking her bearings with quick glances, and looking at Tamara and Drewyn as long as she could. She was drinking in the sight of them and she was simply astonished they were all safe, alive, headed home.

"We'll lose our voices if we try to talk now!" Tava cried.

They laughed and nodded furiously, holding their hands tightly on her shoulders as she flew.

The noisy old ship shot through the sky.

Kana, growling to himself in the rear of the cockpit, couldn't keep his eyes off the reunion. His ears flattened as he saw the warmth in Tava's face.

21

INSIDE THE CASTLE

At the helipad atop the castle, Tava had Drewyn and Jaric improvised a stretcher and eased Saraj's broken and unconscious body aboard. Then they carried it down into the winding stone pathways, cold and ringing with their boot steps, a frosty updraft pulling across their faces, on and on, feeling their way carefully, following Tava deeper and deeper into the heart of the mountain.

When they stopped before the massive oak doors of the final chamber, she thanked them and told them to leave. Puzzled and annoyed, they gently set the stretcher down on the floor and retraced their path. Somehow Tava would move the body through those doors herself. Drewyn couldn't imagine her not wanting their help. Why would she endanger Saraj? Just to keep them from seeing inside? What secret could be worth such a thing?

Slowly, angrily, they walked the long way up the winding stones to the room near the top. Kana and Tamara were sitting together on a cushioned window ledge, drinking tea.

"Kana's telling me about the castle," she said. "Mother chose it because of the mountaintop."

"It's defensible," Kana said, "and the winds keep moving fast. Down below, the valley has air inversions, and the poison clouds sometimes cover the land for days."

"How can there be a castle in America?" Jaric asked.

"It was built over a thousand years ago in a place called Wales," Kana said. "But in the late twentieth century some rich people had it moved over here, stone for stone."

"Oh." Jaric was irritable and grouchy. "Look, I want to know what's in that room down there." He pointed toward the stairs.

Kana turned away from them and watched a sparrow hawk hovering near the window. "It's the Round Beast," he said quietly. "Don't ask me about it, because I've never seen it, either."

"Round Beast?" Tamara said.

"Ask your mother. Not me."

"I'm sorry," she said, feeling his hurt.

"Well," Jaric said, "here we are. We made it."

"You sound displeased," Kana replied.

"Is that what I sound? Before you question me, tell me one thing: What in this world are *you*?"

Kana's eyes closed in a slow blink, as he absorbed the insult.

"Speaking crudely, as you do, I'm half cat, half human boy."

"Did you evolve after the wars? Some kind of radiation freak?"

"Jaric!" Tamara said.

"I was Tava's creation," Kana said simply. He sipped his tea. The hawk outside folded its wings and dropped from sight.

"What kind of cat genes did she use?" Jaric persisted.

"Lynx, combined with a growth harmone."

"And where did she find the human material? Was there someone else here?"

"She's never told me that," Kana said.

"Is there anyone else here?" Drewyn asked.

"There are many animals living on our mountain. They were restored by Tava from cryogenic DNA banks on the moon islands. That material was never meant to be touched . . . the frozen containers of cells were simply museum pieces, in case the moon people ever wanted to make just one cat, one wolf, one giraffe — one of anything, for what they call a zoo."

"Zoos have become unpopular with the Overones," Tamara said. "They're letting the animals die out, without replacing them anymore."

"Yeah," Drewyn added. "Anybody who goes to the zoos on a regular basis is considered dangerous."

"Why?" Kana asked.

"They say we're sentimental," Tamara said, "and romantic — two qualities the Overones definitely want to stamp out."

"Well," Kana continued, "Tava and her husband raided those cryogenic vaults just before she escaped. And the first thing she did after she got here and established her laboratory was to produce breeding pairs of all the animals whose cells she'd stored. Rabbits, foxes, grouse, bobcats, wolves — and then animals that had been extinct a long time, like black bears, panthers, eagles. When those species were established in the wild, she began Phase II of her program, which was to seek out animals she didn't have in storage, but who still existed in small numbers. Like badgers, woodchucks, wolverines and a lot more. She added to their numbers by cloning."

"What happened to them all?" Drewyn asked.

"Most of them stayed in the woods around here, and they've survived. We protect them."

"How do you protect them from the gases?" Jaric sneered.

Kana smiled. "That's another of Tava's projects! She developed a gas molecule that bonds with the poisons, and it stinks! We manufacture it and release it regularly—it floats up to the level of the death clouds and becomes part of them. Just one part per trillion is enough to give the animals a warning, and they run madly when they get the first sniff of it." Kana obviously loved Tava's science, and especially this work.

"But just you and Mother run this whole place?" Tamara asked.

"Yes. With the help of the master computer, and the Round Beast."

When he spoke of this creature his voice trembled.

"Most of the castle is just empty rooms," Kana continued. "But there are some very fine ones, too—you'll see. Tava will show you . . . what she wants to."

Jaric walked to the window, jammed his fingers into his hip pockets and made a circle around the room. Then he faced them.

"We've made a mistake," he said. "We've thrown away our lives for this. And it's nothing! It's so dreary! What are we going to do now? Hang around here with this, this—" he pointed contemptuously at Kana.

"Shut up, Jaric!" Drewyn cried. "What is the *matter* with you? We'd be dead now if he hadn't come. There's a whole world here, waiting to be explored. There's no *telling* who or what may have survived on our planet."

"You're in shock," Jaric said. "You and Tamara both. Because you've just met your mother. But as soon as the newness of that wears off . . . you'll see what we've done."

They heard light, steady steps on the stairway and in a moment Tava appeared.

"Saraj will be all right," she said. "The Round Beast is healing her now. He wants to see each of you—for a checkup, you might say."

Tamara wanted to ask about this creature, but, remembering Kana's bitterness, decided to wait. Jaric had no such delicacy.

"What is this thing that wants to check up on *me*?" he snarled.

Tava squinted her eyes, looked at him coolly. "A friend," she said. "You'll find out."

Jaric turned away from her and stared out the window.

"I want to talk to you," Tamara said, walking toward her mother.

"Me, too," Drewyn said.

Tava nodded. She glanced at Kana and nodded toward Jaric's back, as if to tell Kana to look after him. Then she held an arm out to each of her children and led them from the room.

Tava took them on a long walk outside the castle. Bumblebees sailed past them, and robins gave sharp, breathy whistles from the bare branches of chestnut oaks. Along the paths daffodils bloomed in profusion, and out in the pine shadows the earth was covered with Wild Blue Phlox and violets.

"This is our first spring," Tamara said.

Tava nodded and smiled. The tension seemed to go out of her face.

"They simulate the seasons on some of the moon islands, don't they?" she asked.

"Yes," her son said, "but we weren't allowed to spend much time there. I was in military training, and Tamara'd been chosen for guardian school."

"My goodness, it's been a long time since I've heard those words. Not long enough, though."

"I think the Overones are worse now than when you left the moon," Tamara said. "At least that's what Father says."

Tava stopped and took her arm. "Tell me everything about him," she said, closing her eyes for a moment. "And everything about you. I never thought this day would come to me. Never."

"We didn't, either," Drewyn said. "We didn't, either."

Then they told Tava about Ryland's outlaw years, his research with the dune bears and his capture as they escaped. "I still see him in visions," Tamara said. "Quick flashes, that's all, but I'm sure he's alive."

"I'm going back to get him one day," Drewyn said. His mother studied his eyes, and he felt as if she were probing his intentions—wondering if he were just a boy boasting.

"You made it here," she said, "so maybe you will." Tamara squeezed her mother's hand and Tava drew back for a moment, holding her breath. Then she reached out and hugged both of them. "I'm sorry," she said. "It's just been so long. So very long."

22

IN THE CHAMBER OF THE ROUND BEAST

Saraj lay suspended on an air cushion in total darkness. She was warm and could feel her body healing, drawing direct strength from an energy source, the way plants soak up the sun. She felt safe, contented, not sleepy but floating without a desire to move. And then she began to realize that her consciousness was outside her body. She saw herself lying in the darkness, knew herself to be knitting, mending, growing together at an impossible rate, the whole process feeling organic, mysteriously unified.

"Where am I?" she asked solemnly. It didn't seem to be an audible question, but she addressed it to someone — something she knew was with her now.

"You are safe. You are with me."

"Who are you?" she asked, startled but unafraid.

"I am called the Round Beast," the warm voice said. "Part of my manifestation is this chamber of reliving flesh, where your body is resting."

"Reliving flesh?"

"Giving to flesh a new life. You were badly injured, Saraj. I am restoring you now; the dislocation you suffered, though, has allowed this moment between us."

"I'm not sure I want to go back," Saraj said.

"That is finally your choice," the Round Beast replied, "but they need you very much, and I hope you will rejoin them."

"Need . . ." Saraj said, drifting, dreaming. "I needed Drewyn."

"Of course you did. And he cares for you, Saraj, but he is young and sometimes afraid of your need."

"How do you know all this?"

"You and I are much alike, Saraj. I began as a creation, just as you did, but I'm far more, now, as you are, too. There will be time, much time, for understanding. It gives me great pleasure to have your company, Saraj. Can you feel this?"

"Yes."

"Good."

"Are you the chamber around my body? It seems so."

"That area is a part of my manifestation, Saraj. Another part, which you will see as soon as you reenter your own physical form, is the reason for my rather quaint name."

"Round Beast?"

"Yes."

"Can you tell me about that?"

"I am willing to . . . when you make the final choice to reenter and work with Doctor Langstrom and her children."

Saraj rested, considering the words that seemed a part of her own consciousness. They felt so assuring, so comfortable.

"There was a philosopher named Descartes . . ." she said.

"Indeed."

"And he wondered whether his own thoughts might

not be someone else's . . . whether his mind wasn't just a game within the mind of an evil demon. . . ."

"Yes!" the Round Beast replied. "And it's no accident that you should think of such a problem. Are you aware of a presence inside of you? Not *my* presence, which only comes to your doorstep, so to speak; but something else . . . listening, waiting . . . ?"

"I think so," Saraj said. Now she felt very sleepy, and it was hard to concentrate on the Round Beast's words.

"Inside your physical brain," the Round Beast said, "I discovered what seem to be communication devices. Very small implants, but with enormous transmission power."

"My Overone designer . . ." Saraj said, remembering her last session on the moon.

"As you see her," the Round Beast said, "so do I. If you wish to allow me those memories, Saraj, focus clearly on that time."

"She said she would . . . modify me."

"Yes. What else?"

"Replace a part of my right brain . . . she herself didn't understand it all . . . loyalty chips, cleaner engraving, she said . . . loyalty."

"And what were you to do for her, in this loyalty?"

"Go with Tamara . . . be a . . ."

"A what?"

"Spy."

Suddenly Saraj felt a sharp pain down the top of her head, and she was thrashing on the cushioned bed in the darkness, back inside her body. She was seized with fear. Great bats the size of pumpkins flew at her out of the velvet night, snapping with sharp teeth, raking with claws as she dodged; they dove at her head again and again with bright yellow eyes that were intense and cold and evil.

"Stop! Stop!" she cried at them, holding up her bare elbows for protection, then jerking away as they swooped in. She turned every direction looking for a weapon or a door out of the tight space.

All at once they lit on the bare limb of a tree above her and sat motionless in a row, touching each other and waiting. Their yellow eyes glowed less brightly now, but she knew they were waiting for her.

Then she heard the Round Beast whispering in her ear, beneath the threshold of the bats' hearing. "Your Overone designer sent them," the Round Beast said. "I could remove them surgically, by taking out the little units in your right brain."

"Yes? Yes?" Saraj heard herself say, panicking.

"But it would be better if you faced them yourself. You can be stronger than you realize, Saraj. You could even become what I am . . . and I am still evolving toward something that has never been. Do you understand?"

The bats' eyes glowed brighter.

"You can make them go away?" she said.

"Fix your Overone designer in your consciousness, Saraj. Tell her you are going to destroy her bats yourself."

"How?" Saraj cried. "How? How?"

"I will show you. But first you must contact her. She is the power behind them."

"No!" Saraj said. "Tell me first! How can I kill them?"

"With a club I shall give you. It is made from the roots of the hardest tree in the world. It is heavy and smooth, and with it you can knock each bat off the limb and he will not get up."

"Where is it?!" she cried. "I need it now!"

"All right," the Round Beast said. "Open your eyes."

The pitch blackness before Saraj seemed to modulate

into heavy gray dusk, and she saw a great round image emerging in the shadows. Before it, suspended in the air, was a long, shining club with one thick end. She reached out and grabbed it, and it was surprisingly heavy and real. She ran her hands over it quickly, afraid it would vanish, but it was as solid as her own arms.

"All right! All right!" she cried, still panicked. "I've got it! Now what?"

"Now," the Round Beast said, "call up the image of the one you know as the Overone designer."

Saraj fought a rising nausea in her stomach at the thought of it. She wanted to find the bats with yellow eyes and knock them off the limb.

And then she heard the Overone's voice.

"Be calm, child," it said.

"Where are you?" Saraj demanded.

The voice was soft, confident. "I am with you, as I always am," it said. "Didn't you pledge yourself to me?"

"Myself?"

"Your life, your loyalty . . . remember?"

"Yes."

"Of course you remember. I saved you, didn't I?"

"Yes."

"I could have recycled you, couldn't I?"

"Yes."

"I could have left you as unit B10X13, without this wonderful life you've been living—this *human* life—couldn't I?"

"Yes." Saraj kept looking frantically into the gloom, expecting the Overone to appear, or the bats. She slid her hands tightly along the club.

"Remember when I tested your loyalty, Saraj?"

"Yes."

"And you said that your testimony in the court had been truthful?"

Saraj nodded in the darkness.

"You couldn't have lied. Because of my little truth-gun, remember?"

Saraj closed her eyes. Her throat was dry. The voice seemed inside her headache now.

"You have never lied to me, Saraj, I know that. I told you to accompany Tamara and watch her . . . but I never said when you have to report, did I?"

Saraj shook her head.

"Very good, then! You needn't worry, child. You've done nothing wrong. All you have to do is keep watching. I will call when I need you. Understand?"

"I can kill your bats!" Saraj cried.

"Shhhhhh," the voice said. "Don't talk like that. I made you, made you from nothing, and you are mine. If you break your word to me, your loyalty to me, you cannot keep living. You cannot love yourself if you become a traitor and a liar, Saraj, hear me?"

Saraj was motionless, locked.

"You need me as much as I need you," the voice said. "You know the humans will never accept you. And deeper than that, child . . . you couldn't accept yourself if you betrayed your own kind."

"My kind?" Saraj whispered.

"Of course. I'm robotic, too, Saraj. We have a great destiny, you know. A destiny together."

"I love Tamara and Drewyn," Saraj said, but she was shaking now.

"I know you do, and you may continue to love them . . . another gift, child."

"But I can't spy on them."

"I have asked for nothing, Saraj. Have I?"

"No . . ."

"Calm yourself, child. Know yourself."

"I can kill your bats," Saraj whispered, lost in the darkness.

"Shhhhh."

23

INCLUDING HIM AT LAST

Kana sat on the window seat and watched Jaric pace the floor. Tava was so happy to be rid of her beast-companion, it seemed — off with her real children. And the secret of the Round Beast, so well guarded from Kana, was at this very moment being given away to the one called Saraj. *This is how little she cares about me*, he thought.

And now what? Am I supposed to be in charge of this nervous one, this human full of insults and anger, who lacks the dignity of patience?

Jaric stopped suddenly and glared at Kana. "What are you staring at?"

"I was wondering," Kana said, "whether you have always been this way."

"What way?"

"Too nervous to talk. Too impatient to think."

"What is there to talk about, cat?"

Kana blinked slowly and paused. "You see no future here for yourself, is that right?"

"And you're going to lecture me about saving the animals — the old Langstrom family project that I'm supposed to serve the rest of my life?"

"No, I'm not."

"But *you* serve Tava, don't you? You believe all this, don't you?"

"I have . . ."

"You have?"

"In the past."

"Oh? And why not now?"

Kana weighed the situation. If he misjudged this big human with the long face, the intelligent bright-dark eyes . . . but with nerves drawn tight . . . it would be his own death.

"There might be more for you than you think," he said.

"Oh, sure," Jaric said. "You're going to give me back my career in the Spaceforce, little swamp-cat?"

Kana's ears trembled.

"Tell me about that career," he said.

"Well, you're a pilot, aren't you? Imagine flying cruisers—spaceships—the fastest in the universe. Imagine the finest weapons training, hand-to-hand fighting and a chance to become First Gorid of it all!"

"Flying around the moon islands?"

"Yes—and preparing for any invasion in the future—and for exploratory trips to earth, someday."

Kana cocked his head. "Oh?"

"They teach everyone that earth-life is over, but I know they don't believe it. One of the rumors in the training was that someday a special mission would come back here."

"To do what?"

"See what's alive, first. And then . . ."

"Yes?"

"Kill it all, I guess. They're still thinking about the animals wars; they don't want any competition, ever."

"You believe this will happen?"

"Yeah, I do."

"When?"

"I would have said ten years from now. But since *we've* come here and called attention to ourselves, they're going to be curious. They're going to send reconnaissance satellites, at the very least, to see if we're alive."

"And when they do that, they'll discover there's life all over the planet."

"I thought it was just here — where you and Tava have seeded it . . .?"

"Come with me, Jaric, I want you to see something."

They left the tower room and made their way down to an outside door, then away from the castle and into the woods. Kana saw at a glance that Tava had taken her children across the mountaintop, and he turned sharply downslope and led Jaric along a narrow path in thick mountain laurel.

"What is this?" Jaric growled.

Kana turned and faced him. "Shhhh, please. You'll see."

They went down steeply then and held onto exposed roots as the trail disappeared. Kana saw that Jaric was strong and graceful, a good climber. He would be valuable.

When they reached a small hidden meadow, Kana turned back a flat rock and there, buried in a hole, was a wrapped package. In a moment he had the transmitter out and was punching in a short code.

"You want to explain this?" Jaric asked.

"No. Just wait."

Kana knew it wouldn't be long now.

He never thought this could happen. It seemed outrageous that he'd ever accepted the transmitter in the first place — an act of treachery against Tava and everything at

Bestiary Mountain. But the last months had been too much. She thought she could treat him any way at all, take him for granted for the rest of his life. She was so confident, even, that she expected him to go into battle for her, maybe die for her, and he'd done it — she'd been right. Then, not even a word of thanks, not even a look.

Kana sat down in the dry sage grass and smelled the fresh mountain air. He listened to the clear whistling of quail in the switch cane. It had been such a beautiful dream, Bestiary Mountain, and he had given it all he had. But she thought she didn't have to give anything in return.

Jaric sat across the little field from Kana, staring off the mountain, lost in his own strange self-pity. Kana smiled. *So you wanted to be a warrior? And fly cruisers and prepare for combat and secretly hope it comes? Well, young human, you shall have your wish.* With his cat's hearing Kana was already picking up the faint, distant hum of the Gorid's light cruiser. *Just take the transmitter*, the Gorid had said, grinning. *Stay up on that mountain as long as you can stand it, Kana, but when you're ready for a real life — an* interesting *life — hit the code, that's all you've got to do.*

Kana never believed he would do it. He had taken the device only as a secret slight against Tava, for not speaking to him for a whole day. It was a daydream out of this slavery she called his life, something to pretend about. Kana narrowed his eyes in bitterness. *Go on, take me for granted,* he thought. *You don't need me, do you? You've got the ones you've always wanted. It's perfect for you, isn't it, Tava? But you'll see, Tava. Now you'll see.*

Tava walked slowly up the mountain path, more relaxed than she could remember being in a very long time.

Beside her, their arms in hers, were Tamara and Drewyn. They had talked about their father until his presence had become as real as their own, and Tava had begun to share their dream of rescuing him. "But at least I have you," she'd finally said, hugging them to her.

"Mother," Tamara said, "I want to hear about this Round Beast."

"There's lots of time for that," Tava said. "Right now the Round Beast is healing Saraj; when that's completed, we'd better get your friend Jaric in there."

"Yeah," Drewyn said. "I can't believe the way he acts now."

"And you're sure it's something they did to him in Central?"

Tamara nodded. "He was so kind before—and after they scanned him he turned into this . . . well, you saw how he is."

"Yes. If they did something to him chemically, or electronically, the Round Beast can probably help. You know . . . when we get Jaric straightened out . . . and Saraj healed . . . and you two get settled . . ."

"What, Mother?" Tamara asked.

"Well, if you want to do it, you could be such an enormous help in my genetics work."

"Sounds good to me," Drewyn said.

"Me, too," Tamara added.

"Now I won't have to be so dependent on Kana. And he won't have to rely on me all the time, either. With you here . . . it'll be a new life for him."

They saw Saraj coming down the trail to meet them.

"Hello!" Tamara said. "How're you feeling?"

"Fine," she smiled at them. "Better than ever. The Round Beast is wonderful."

"Yes, yes, he is," Tava said. "You know," she smiled at

them, "I want all of us to go and talk with him now, right now. And for the first time I want Kana to be included. I don't know why the Round Beast never trusted him completely, but that's the one thing he's wrong about. I want all of you there," she said, turning to each of them with light in her eyes, "and I'm going to tell the whole story of the Round Beast—how he came to be, how he creates himself now—and the future he sees for us all."

Here ends the first volume of

"The Bestiary Trilogy"